When Love Danced

A Novel
by
Mukai Heather Jaravaza

ISBN: 979-8-9926258-0-6 (paperback)
ISBN: 979-8-9926258-2-0 (E-book)
Certified under US Copyright Office in accordance with title 17
This is an original work of fiction. All references to historical events, real places and real people are used factiously. All characters, organizations and events portrayed in this novel are either a product of the author's imagination or used fictitiously.
Front Cover Image by Aissata Yacouba
www.JosephMukai.store
Printed by Joseph&Mukai Business LLC in the United States of America
First printing edition 2025.
Joseph&Mukai Business
1849 South Road, #1017, Wappinger Falls, NY 12590

When Love Danced

Chapter One
Foundation: Daniel's Poem

"Before I met you, Danai, I loved you!" Daniel murmured to himself. He grimaced at summer's oppressive heat. A subtle breeze tickled his lips. He shifted uncomfortably, remembering the first time he'd laid eyes on the unusual girl.

It had been a day like today. Arthur agreed to meet him outside Ricky's Ice Cream Shack, but as usual, his cousin had been late. Daniel stood at the edge of the ice cream courtyard, silently cursing his cousin's tardiness. His gaze fell on three girls seated at a wooden table. A girl in a red minidress leaned over the tottering table and unabashedly licked her friend's ice cream cone. Bewildered, her friend pushed the girl away, but the daring girl tried a second time. Ice cream on her tongue, she burst into a smile and laughed triumphantly.

"Danai, stop!" her friend protested. Reaching toward the sky, the girl's arms shook in victory. She rose from her seat and began dancing, her hips rhythmically twirling and twisting to the beat of her rebellion.

Daniel laughed at her friend's baffled expression. Aroused with curiosity, his eyes trailed the contours of the mischievous girl's apple-shaped face. Her stubborn cheekbones arched firmly beneath small almond eyes. His gaze rested on her voluptuous lips smudged in deep red lipstick. From across the courtyard, Daniel watched and saw only her. In that moment, he had known this girl was created to be his.

"Hey, I'm here." Arthur stumbled through a growing crowd, pulling Daniel out of thoughts of the past and back into the present. "What's got you so caught up? You didn't even hear me calling." Arthur's eyes followed his cousin's gaze toward a cluster of girls gathered around DJ Tonite's turntables. His attention fell on the girl dressed in a cropped stonewashed jacket.

"Hey, isn't that the girl from Ricky's Ice Cream Shack two months ago?" He grinned at the girl's tiny denim skirt revealing her shapely cinnamon legs. "That's her, right? Hey, man, you should go talk to her." Arthur led his cousin farther into Suzette's backyard.

"Suzette, I'm sorry I'm late." Arthur jerked around to embrace a girl creeping up behind him.

"You're always late, Arthur." Suzette pouted and wrapped her arms around Arthur's waist. "How can you be late for my birthday? When are you going to grow up?"

"You know I'm trying, babe." He wiped the sweat gathering on his forehead and shoved a sloppily wrapped gift box into his girlfriend's hands. "Do you know how much I love you? Happy birthday, Suzy."

2

Oblivious to Authur and Suzette's flirtatious banter, Daniel watched the girl in the denim skirt. Two months ago, he'd been afraid to speak to her, but today Daniel felt new. "My entire life depends on this moment," he mumbled to himself, gliding toward the group of girls.

"Will you dance with me?" Daniel held out his hand. His eyes flickered to Arthur laughing in the distance.

"What?" Danai stared at the boy standing before her. Her eyes trailed down his overwashed jeans to the worn-out sandals.

"I want to dance with you," the lanky boy whispered, placing his hand in hers. Despite her friends' collective murmuring, Danai followed him to the dance floor. They moved awkwardly until Daniel set the pace, and the first song merged into the next.

Years before Danai and Daniel's paths first crossed, Daniel had become entrapped in an average existence. He couldn't remember if he chose it or it chose him. The first child of an ordinary couple who'd birthed typical dreams—a comfortable house in a nice neighborhood, a large backyard and two children—Daniel Munya Tashaya attended conventional schools and made unremarkable friends. By the time puberty arrived, he'd adopted a mediocre personality to match the commonness suffocating him. "Dependable!" He chuckled at his mother's description of him.

Startled, Danai's eyes flickered. That's when Daniel saw it—the something he couldn't explain. Danai giggled, and Daniel grinned giddily. The soft melody of her laughter ripped through him and settled into his core. The second song faded away.

"Thank you." She pulled her hand out of his grasp.

3

"There's this new movie, *Do the Right Thing*," he blurted out. "If you're free next Saturday, maybe we could see it together."

"I don't know you." Confusion covered Danai's face.

"A friend of mine works at Rainbow Movie Theaters, and he got me free tickets," he lied. His voice trailed off as he glanced at her friends laughing in the distance. "And I want to see it with you."

The sincerity in the boy's eyes stole Danai's attention. Reaching into a pink clutch, she pulled out an old piece of newspaper and scribbled her phone number. She shoved it into his pocket before rushing back to her friends.

She's forgotten me even before I introduced myself. Daniel watched the rhythmic sway of Danai's hips as she walked away.

"Arthur," he hollered.

"What?"

"I feel average dying and the beginning of something new," Daniel shouted. Both boys turned to gawk at the girl swaying in the distance.

Chapter Two
"Say Something"

"Yes, I'm the man, and I'm stepping out to meet the woman of my dreams," Daniel announced to his younger brother while spraying Palmer's Oil Sheen onto his fresh box cut. "Saturday, March eighteenth, 1989. Man, I will never forget this day." He grinned at a coffee-stained calendar on his dresser and shifted his attention back to the mirror reflection of himself in his favorite outfit: stone-washed jeans, a black Run-DMC T-shirt, and sky-blue Reebok high-tops. He grabbed a jacket off the dresser and rushed out of the door.

Drenched in anticipation of Spike Lee's new joint, young and old couples, crews in their best gear, and the occasional lone person clamored as they headed into Rainbow Movie Theater. The crowd appeared intoxicated with expectancy. Daniel clutched his tickets and waded through the swarm. He stood next to an elderly man at the entrance and waited for Danai. Electrified by the atmosphere, Daniel barely noticed the first hour come and go. A group of bystanders migrated to a nearby Bhawa to have a beer or two. The mass gathering dispersed into the aging theater, and Daniel frantically searched the dwindling crowd.

Do The Right Thing began, but Danai was nowhere in sight.

Daniel stood at the theater entrance until the day's heat became unbearable. An uncomfortable nakedness of rejection crept through his body. Summer's midday sun disappeared into a darkening sky. Heaven opened her mouth and soaked the earth with tears of rain. Alarmed by the rain's intensity, a heavyset woman grabbed her child and dashed toward a nearby shelter. In her haste, the woman fell onto Daniel, hurling both him and her child into gushing waters. Soaked in humiliation, Daniel rose up and trudged back home.

"I will never wait for you again, Danai," he yelled at the turbulent sky as he shoved open the familiar pink rusty gate. The boisterous rain abruptly stopped, and summer's sun reappeared as if she'd never left. Daniel stared at retreating clouds in confusion. On Saturday, March eighteenth, 1989, Daniel Munya Tashaya walked into the Tashaya home and quietly stepped back into the suffocating confines of an ordinary life.

"It's been *two weeks* since that girl stood you up. Get over it, man." Arthur barged into Daniel's bedroom and stared at the mess of unworn clothes strewn around the room. Daniel lay sprawled on his bed with his head buried under the blanket.

"Cousin, I'm taking you down under to Sarchies today." Arthur ignored his cousin's disheveled appearance and chuckled at his bewildered expression.

Sarchies, a rite of passage for Harare's cool crowd. An exclusive nightclub located in the hidden underground of Harare's prestigious Business District. At night, the club hosted shady events, but on Friday and Saturday afternoons, it catered to teenagers. However, the club's teens-only afternoon policy couldn't deter party-hungry university students or the disgruntled young adult working crowd. It was common to see a fifty-year-old sugar daddy searching for his fourth or fifth wife.

"Today you'll finally enter Arthur's kingdom." Arthur gulped down a glass of Mazowe juice. Daniel frowned at his cousin's description of the infamous joint. Ripe with dubious transactions, dealers used Sarchies' loud music and dim lights to camouflage their illegal activities. Dressed in elegant Pierre Cardin suits, these gentlemen of the streets engaged in everything from money laundering to luxury vehicle theft and sales. Despite the club's popularity and large weekly turnout, admittance was by invite only. A member had to invite and bring you in, vouching for your presence. No one really understood how anyone became a member, but the huge bouncers seemed to instinctively know who not to let in. Daniel vividly remembered a rumor of a girl who had been stabbed by an angry ex-lover in Sarchies. The incident took place publicly on the dance floor. When the police arrived, not one witness could be found. What happened in Sarchies stayed in Sarchies.

"So, you coming, man?" Arthur stuck his head out of the kitchen.

"Yes. I'm coming," Daniel conceded.

Dressed in black pleated pants and shiny patent leather shoes, the boys arrived in Harare's Business District shortly after noon. Arthur scrutinized his cousin and laughed. Both cousins were good-looking seventeen-year-olds but exact opposites. At five foot ten, Daniel was tall, dark, and athletically built. Shorter and stouter in stature, Arthur's round face was interrupted by a single dimple. Their differences extended to their personalities. Always popular, Arthur remained outgoing while Daniel's presence tended to go unnoticed.

"Masikati. How can I help you today?" asked a petite young woman dressed in an elaborate emerald-green suit. She sat behind a desk.

"Arthur Rwizi and guest. We are going down under," Arthur announced.

The woman pulled out a massive logbook and scanned through its withered pages. "Go ahead." She pressed a buzzer, and Daniel followed Arthur down a spiral of marble stairs. As the boys descended the stairs, they were met by the sounds of De La Souls' "Eye Know." Their journey ended at two mahogany doors flanked by four burly bouncers.

"Ah, this is Daniel. He's cool." Arthur slid the four-dollar cover charge through a small peephole. "I'm bringing him in."

An elderly white lady sat on the other side of the hole. She stuck out her hand to grab the money and stamp each boy's hand.

"Welcome down under, cousin," Arthur shouted. The bouncers opened the doors. "Welcome to Arthur's kingdom," Arthur laughed.

Elaborately furnished with black leather sofas, dark carpets, and elegant mahogany tables, Sarchies held a sense of grandeur. Daniel's eyes rapidly assessed his new surroundings. The club's classic decoration sharply contrasted beams of colorful illuminating lights that

8

danced in tune with the music. Together it created an appealing ambience, and Daniel instinctively knew he wanted to stay.

Smoke lingered, creating an atmosphere of mystery. Amid the teens' familiar faces were dealers with their girlfriends, as well as the entire St. Vincent High basketball team dressed in their customary red, gray, and white. Pretty girls in colorful outfits filled every corner. A pregnant girl breezed past as she led her partner to the dance floor, and Daniel followed Arthur, attempting to look like he belonged.

"Hey, look, there's the Richlorne crew." Arthur rushed toward the VIP seating area. Known as the Richlorne crew after the high school they attended, the group of boys ran Harare's party scene. Nyika Tumai, the group's leader, stood in the center talking to a tall girl with a short, cropped afro. The ebony beauty wore a tight-fitting short pink dress. Her rhinestone-studded heels exaggerated her height. She appeared engrossed in every word Nyika spoke.

"Hey, Nyika, this is my cousin, Danny," Arthur blurted.

The girl frowned at the unwelcome intrusion. Nyika Tumai grinned and nodded briefly before returning to his conversation with the ebony beauty. Arthur led Daniel farther into the VIP area. The rest of the Richlorne crew sat on the leopard skin couches—Godfrey, Derek Love, Will B., and of course, Makhosini Moyo. While the boys sipped on Fantas and nodded to De La Soul's "Eye Know," Makhosini's attention remained glued on something in the distance. Mesmerized and motionless, the boy gaped toward the opposite end of the club. Daniel's eyes followed Makhosini's gaze, and there she was: Danai.

Danai looked different. She'd shaved the left side of her head. The remaining hair extensions fell like a waterfall of flowing curls. Draped in a long purple dress, she moved like the wind. The music swirled, and Danai followed in twirls. The two slits on her dress opened to reveal weathered, stonewashed jeans and shiny black lace-up schoolboy shoes. The beat rocked. Danai spun. Her feet moved to every bounce of the music. Despite the club's dim ambiance, the crowd froze in awe. Oblivious to the appreciative stares, Danai flowed like a waterfall. Her arms gracefully rose upward, seeming to capture each delicious sound.

When the song ended, she simply left the dance floor and sat on a couch next to one of her friends. Daniel glanced back at Makhosini, whose attention was elsewhere. Still captivated, Daniel glided toward Danai.

"Hi," he blurted.

Surprised, Danai glanced up at the lanky boy in a Run-DMC T-shirt. She burst into a fit of giggles. Daniel grinned and forgot he'd ever stood in the rain waiting for her.

Chapter Three
Invitation

"Where are we going?" Danai shouted, twirling on the street corner. Her eyes slanted to avoid summer's piercing sun rays, and Daniel laughed. "Is that for me?" she asked.

A vision of Arthur's expression when he'd confessed that he'd asked Danai out again floated through his mind. *Be careful, man.* His cousin's warning resonated in his thoughts.

Daniel had arrived early for their date, carrying a blossoming blue orchid. To his delight, Danai showed up on time this time.

"Is that for me?" she asked again.

"Yes."

"I love orchids." She beamed in delight and hugged the miniature pot. "Thank you, Daniel."

"Follow me, Miss Matamba." He grabbed her hand and led the way to the spectacular, newly renovated Flame Lilly Inn.

"I keep hearing this song everywhere." Danai settled into a booth by the window.

"Oh, that's 'The Way Love Is' by Ten City. That whole album is totally off the wall," Daniel said, sitting opposite her. "It's about this guy and girl who meet. They fall in love and promise each other forever. The crazy part is that things go wrong. Their love suddenly dies, and they go separate ways."

"Really." Danai watched him carefully. "Have you ever been in love?"

"No, not yet." Daniel grinned. "And you? Am I going to be your first love?"

"What?" She erupted in laughter. They launched into a discussion on love and music: the greatest hits, missed number ones, and the songs they both thought were simply overrated. A waitress appeared and took their orders.

"So, Daniel, what do you do for fun?"

"Well, there's not much to tell," he mumbled. His ordinary existence flickered through his mind. "What about you? Do you have any siblings?"

"I do." Danai smiled, ignoring his forlorn expression, "I have a nine-year-old brother, Miles. He's my cuddly annoyance."

They ate in silence with Daniel peering over his food at Danai, while she glared at other patrons. Despite her enjoying her food, the delicious meal was marked with an awkward tension. Determined to lighten the mood, Daniel joked about a date he had gone on a month earlier.

"So, she showed up an hour late with five of her friends. Before I sat down, her five friends had picked out the most expensive things on the menu and were demanding I pay for their meals." Daniel shook his head, laughing. "So, I sat down, quickly gulped down my meal, and then I snuck out through the back door." He chuckled at his own ingenuity.

Danai frowned but nodded silently.

"So, Danai, what do you think about me?" He nervously swallowed.

Danai slowly chewed. "I think you're being a typical seventeen-year-old boy."

"What do you mean?"

"You're very predictable." Her eyes wandered from his gaze to his plate.

"Well, I am an average guy." He shifted uncomfortably. "So, what are you saying?"

"I'm saying that it's a hot day but you had us walk up and down First Street for an hour so everyone would see us." She played with a roasted potato. "Now you are telling me about some girl I'll probably never meet. That's typical." She lifted her knife and sliced her potato into tiny pieces. They ate the rest of the meal in silence.

"Okay, so why don't you pick the next place we go to?" Daniel suggested as they left Flame Lilly Inn. "Maybe we could do something not typical." Despite Danai's earlier comments, he'd enjoyed their date and wanted to see her again.

"Daniel, you really seem like a nice guy, but I don't think this is for me. I . . ."

"I like you, Danai." He nervously ran his fingers through his hair. "A lot."

"I think you like the idea of us."

"Yes, I like that, too. I want everything, girl." He grinned at her expression. "Give me one more chance. We'll go where you want to go and do something you like. And if it doesn't work out, then we'll just go separate ways."

The following Saturday, Daniel rushed into Rick's Ice Cream Shack and found Danai waiting for him.

"Hi." She waved and adjusted the strap on her faded indigo-wash overalls. "Are you ready, Danny?"

Weaving through streams of pedestrians while avoiding traffic, Daniel followed Danai past several high-rise buildings. At the entrance of the overly populated Material District, Danai stood on the edge of a curb and stuck out her thumb. A speeding minivan came to a halt.

"Come on, let's go." She pushed into the crowded van.

Daniel squeezed between a large woman in a tight orange skirt and a young schoolboy. "Where are we going?" Daniel asked.

"Mbare. Mbare Musika. Let's go," bellowed the boy who manned the door. The boy stuck half his body out of the moving vehicle and continued shouting at anyone walking in the direction the van was heading.

Mbare Musika! Was this one of Danai's silly pranks? Daniel's unanswered question sparked internal panic.

Built during the oppressive segregation era of colonization, Mbare lay at the city's outskirts. Initially a close-knit settlement for migratory farmers, Mbare transformed into a bustling bus center built to transport Black people to any part of the country they worked. Within weeks, multiple food stands appeared. With the stands came eager street vendors who sold everything from ladies' shoes and children's clothing to farming equipment. Amid the confusion, a massive flourishing marketplace erupted, and the tiny settlement transformed into a thriving township.

Despite the end of colonialism and several changes in the country, Mbare remained standing: solid and proud. Mbare's doctors and professors moved to more affluent suburbs, and the once attractive surroundings deteriorated into decaying apartment flats that housed everything from struggling families to seasoned thieves. People were born in Mbare, and they died in Mbare. That was the story of their life. Like most suburban teens in Zimbabwe, Daniel had heard about Mbare Musika but never been there. He was surprised Danai knew how to get there.

"Give me your wallet, Daniel." Danai held out her hand as the minivan came to a halt. Danai paid the boy who manned the door, and Daniel followed her out of the van into the unruly marketplace. His eyes danced at the sights surrounding him: women selling vegetables, new and used clothes, curtains, and handcrafted furniture.

"Come and buy them now. They'll be gone tomorrow!" A man enticed customers. Daniel grinned at the man's brazen display of the latest BeatBoxes. Old women purchased sewing machines, and young mothers bought their weekly food supply. A group of enthusiastic tourists bargained with a vendor for his overpriced glistering Shona sculptures, and a savvy businessman grinned triumphantly as he rushed past the couple.

Danai stopped at a staggering hut with corroding metal roofing and read the rusty blackboard: "Alice's Shabeen." The hut's entrance gave a clear view of metal plates, jars of spices, and preserved foods. Outside, thirty wooden crates had been converted into seats for customers. A large firewood stove with black pots lay in the center. A woman wiped her sooty hands on her worn apron and greeted Danai.

"This is Mai Chenai," Danai told Daniel. "Or Alice. She's the owner." She handed Mai Chenai fifty cents, and the woman hurried into the hut, opened a mini fridge, and returned with bottles of ginger ale and cherry plum.

Around the shabeen's periphery, African batiks, oil paintings, and other pieces of art hung on chicken wire fence.

"So, what do you think?" Danai pointed to a medium-sized painting depicting a peaceful village setting. In the center of the serene setting stood a young girl in a tattered green dress defiantly holding a book.

Daniel walked up to the oil painting and took a closer look. The artist had inscribed her name at the bottom of the canvas. "You did this?" he blurted in astonishment.

"Yes, I did!" Danai giggled. "I bring my stuff here. Cautious, Mai Chenai's oldest son, collects and sells art. He sells some of my paintings."

Upon hearing his name, Cautious suddenly appeared. Dressed in a wrinkled shirt and unwashed jeans, he stood glaring suspiciously at Daniel.

16

Ignoring Cautious, Danai asked, "Daniel, are you hungry?"

"Yeah, I am."

"Okay, come. Let's eat."

They joined twenty other guests seated on crates. A teenage girl wearing a sauce-stained apron hovered over everyone. Pouring water into a basin, she allowed each customer to wash their hands. Mai Chenai followed, unloading bowls of steaming sadza and steak into her customers' hungry hands. As Daniel became aware of the inviting spicy aroma, he heard his stomach growl in anticipation. He reached for one of Mai Chenai's bowls and gulped down his sadza. The simple meal was delicious.

A man in a faded sky-blue suit leaned over and declared, "A steak is never a steak without *Chibuku*." He handed Daniel a container of Mai Chenai's thick brown homemade brew. Daniel took a sip and passed it to Danai.

She frowned and stared at the container. "Nope, and if you're clever, you won't either."

While the customers dug into their meals, the man in the faded blue suit began his story. Everyone listened and occasionally commented as the man talked about his woes and the battles between his two wives. In a relaxed mood, he recounted how he met and fell in love with his first wife. "We were like you two." The man pointed at Daniel and Danai. "I was seventeen, and she was just fifteen. I knew she was the one the first time I laid eyes on her." The man smiled and reminisced about how they left the village and moved to the city. He began working for a manufacturing company, and his wife became a schoolteacher. The years unfolded with promotion after promotion

17

until he became the company's general manager. "Sometimes life doesn't work out the way you plan it." The man shook his head and chuckled. A few customers nodded in agreement. "I felt I needed to take on a second wife. It was an act of mercy. I wanted to share the wealth," the man declared, and the crowd convulsed with laughter.

"I'm a prisoner." Lucky Dube's melodious voice penetrated through Mai Chenai's wireless radio. "I'm a prisoner," Lucky moaned. The man in the blue suit gulped his Chibuku and shook his head at the irony.

"I married for love." A disheveled woman in a traditional head scarf settled onto a crate and began her story. "My mother and aunts warned me to marry in wisdom, but I scoffed at their foolishness and married for love. My husband and I, we started out that way, with me loving him and him simply living in the moment." The woman adjusted her head wrap while the crowd hummed in anticipation.

"To make love work, I worked hard as a housemaid. Cleaning other people's bedrooms and chasing after their insolent children while my own home remained unkept, and my daughters grew up seeing their mother once a month." The woman laughed boldly, exposing a missing tooth. Surprised, Daniel moved closer.

"I'm a grown woman but every day I bow to women younger than me. I call them Madame, and they label me girl." The woman's voice trailed off as the crowd quivered in bitterness. Mai Chenai moved around, discretely serving each customer while the crowd continued listening intently.

"I didn't mind because I married for love. While my husband gambled our meager savings and neglected our home, I woke up each

18

day and kept bowing to those young girls who'd married in wisdom." The woman rose to her feet. With her hands clasping her head, she slowly paced between the crates.

"Last week, my husband's family came to visit our home. They brought a young girl in her twenties. I rejoiced, believing they'd finally heard my pain and brought me my own housemaid. I eagerly sat on the floor and served my in-laws. 'You can rest now,' my father-in-law cheered and ate greedily. 'You birthed four beautiful girls, but we need a son. We've bought a new madam for your home to take on that task.' Astonished, I turned to my husband, and that's when I realized, I'd married for love, and he was now happily living in this moment."

"Oh no, what to do?" The crowd's muffled dismay filtered the woman's agony.

Defeated, the woman dropped to the ground and sat in the dust.

"How can this be?" An elderly man leaned on his cane and angrily spat into the air. Customers shook their heads and resumed eating in silence.

Breaking the silence, a different person shared his own story, while a separate group formed to discuss Zimbabwe's current politics. Daniel listened and giggled. He'd forgotten his surroundings. He felt strangely comfortable and was enjoying himself. He felt good, like he was floating.

"That's the Chibuku." He heard Danai's warning. "And it's getting dark. Time to go." She rose from her crate and handed Mai Chenai the dollars for their meal.

"How much for this one?" Daniel motioned to Cautious and pointed at Danai's work of art.

"Thirty dollars."

"What? Cautious, have you lost your mind?" Mai Chenai's head swerved toward her son. "Do you want me to interrupt your stupidity with a good slap?"

"Twenty dollars," the young man conceded.

"Give me my wallet," Daniel ordered Danai. He pulled out his last note and handed it to Cautious.

"Hey, man, wake up. Wake up, man. We're here!" A male voice dragged Daniel out of his sleep. He grudgingly opened his eyes. Slouched in the back seat of a taxi, he clung to the painting of the girl in the green dress but couldn't find his wallet or Danai.

"I think I was robbed," Daniel stuttered in embarrassment as he slid out of the taxicab, "I'll pay you tomorrow," he assured the taxi driver, who hurled angry insults. Ignoring the driver's threats, he staggered through the rusty pink gate and into his home. Confused but still hugging his painting, he walked past his parents and into his bedroom. With Danai's art propped on his chest, Daniel dropped onto his bed and fell back asleep.

Chapter Four
Whatever Makes You Happy

"Daniel, it's almost noon!" Mrs. Tashaya inspected her lethargic son sprawled on the ruffled duvet. "Are you sick? You've been lying in that bed since yesterday."

"Yes. I mean, no. I'm not sick, Amai," Daniel groaned. His entire body ached. He felt like he'd been in a fight and lost. Silently battling nausea, Daniel rolled over and groaned a second time. *A meal is never a meal without Chibuku*, the man in the blue suit had insisted.

"You have a call." Amai frowned, "I'll tell them to call back tomorrow."

"Yes, Amai." He rolled over again and floated back to sleep.

"Amai, who called earlier?" Daniel entered the kitchen later that afternoon.

"Some girl! How are you feeling? Did you eat something bad?"

Before Daniel could reply, the phone rang a second time.

21

"Hi, Daniel." Danai sounded lively. "Where do you live?"

"What?" He stared at the receiver in disbelief.

"Where do you live? I'm coming over."

"Amai, a friend of mine wants to come over."

"What friend?" His mother's large hands gripped her hips. She moved closer to her son. "No, you were vomiting in the bathroom earlier. Your friend can come over another time."

"But Amai, it'll be just for a few minutes. We have to do something for school," he lied and then rushed toward the bathroom.

An hour later, Danai stood outside the rusty pink gate. "This is yours." She grinned and handed him his wallet.

Daniel carefully inspected its contents. Satisfied, he looked up to see Amai standing by the kitchen door, peering at them.

"Hey, would you like to take a walk and see my neighborhood?" He strategically avoided his mother's gaze.

"Sure." Danai smiled and followed him onto a quiet side street.

"I feel like crap, but I have to admit I had fun yesterday," Daniel confessed.

"Yeah, I noticed the camaraderie between you and Cautious." Danai laughed, following him off the tar road. They strolled beneath rows of blossoming mango trees.

"I like your neighborhood." Danai surveyed the street of gated houses with well-kept gardens. The quiet suburb held an appealing ambiance. "What do you do for fun?"

"Nothing really. Mostly I just hang out at home with my younger brother. Sometimes one of my boys will stop by. You see the lime green house over there." He pointed. "That's my boy Jimmy Lee's

22

home. If you walk down that lane, there's a canteen at Belvedere shopping center. On Saturdays, the neighborhood kids hang out there."

Stopping by a travelling ice cream man, he bought a strawberry milkshake and handed it to Danai. "So, Danai, how do I become your man?" Daniel surprised himself with his question.

"Just ask and we'll see." She laughed mischievously.

Daniel continued walking in silence.

"Well, aren't you going to ask?" she asked.

"No, I'm waiting for the perfect time."

"Typical!" Danai shook her head in humor.

"Whatever!" Daniel laughed. "Whatever, Danai." He leaned over and kissed the arch of her jaw. In an instant, all traces of his headache vanished. Filled with joy, Daniel pulled her closer and kissed her full lips.

Gently pushing him away, she broke the kiss and ran between luscious mango trees. Daniel laughed loudly and boldly chased the girl of his dreams. The sky thundered, releasing showers of rain. Cool water soaked everything in sight, and Danai giggled as she sprinted between budding mango trees. Water rushed through the neighborhood, sweeping away all remnants of yesterday's heatwave. When he caught up with her, they held each other and swayed to the rain's rhythmic music.

I really don't want this girl to leave, I'm really starting to like her. Daniel thought. He stood in the distance and watched Danai waiting to board a rickety minivan at the taxi depot.

A heavyset woman grabbed her wailing child and dashed toward the van. The woman stumbled. To Daniel's amazement, Danai arched to avoid the falling woman and landed on her feet, catching both the woman and her baby.

"Danai, are you okay?" he called.

"Yes."

"Will you be my girlfriend?" Daniel hollered through the crowd, "Girl, I wanna be your man."

"Yes." She giggled at the lanky boy shouting in the distance.

"Yes!" He triumphantly jumped. "Goodnight, Danai Matamba."

"Goodnight, Daniel Tashaya."

Chapter Five
Devotion

1989 was the year of transformation. In January 1989, FW De Klerk announced that he would be replacing Pik Botha as South Africa's National Party Leader, a move that accelerated the already public demise of apartheid. Later that month, Bobby Brown stepped out of the shadows of New Edition. Bobby openly declared his newfound freedom with "My Prerogative." The hit single topped the Billboard Music Charts for weeks. In the year of transformation, Kareem Abdul-Jabbar became the first NBA player to score thirty-eight thousand points. Later that year, he would play his last game as a Laker. In Eastern Europe, protestors frantically chipped away the twenty-eight-year-old Berlin wall, propelling the fall of the USSR—and the world transformed herself.

For Daniel Tashaya, 1989 was the year they became "Daniel and Danai" and he finally escaped his prison of average. He proudly introduced Danai to his boys. They liked her. Today, Danai insisted that he meet her friends.

"I'm sorry we're late," Danai apologized to three girls slouched in a booth. She flopped into a seat next to Thulani. "Oh, guys, this is Daniel."

"We've been waiting for two hours, Danai," Sibo protested, ignoring the boy standing at the opposite end of their table. The other girls nodded in unison. Glancing briefly at the lanky boy, the girls frowned before resuming an earlier conversation. A faint chill washed through Daniel's body. He'd been assessed and silently dismissed.

"Guys, I'm really sorry," Danai mumbled. "We got stuck in traffic."

"That's okay, Danai. We were actually about to leave," Layla remarked. She rose from her seat, threw a five-dollar bill on the table, and left. Within minutes, the other two girls muttered excuses and followed suit.

"Just ignore them!" Danai said as she and Daniel left the restaurant. "I guess they feel like I'm spending too much time with you and not enough time with them. You understand, right?"

"Yes, okay." Daniel nodded. In truth, he couldn't digest the arrogance of her snobbish friends, but he knew he liked Danai. "It's cool!"

A new school semester began. Daniel returned to Sabersvale High, and Danai left for boarding school. To fill the void of her absence, Daniel engaged in the art of letter writing. While his letters were elaborate and descriptive, Danai's replies tended to be shorter, highlighting the mundane day-to-day events of boarding school. She preferred calling from a nearby public phone. He created a mixtape, his version of the Quiet Storm love grooves. They chose Luther's "If This World Were Mine" as their song. A week later, a large teddy bear arrived in the mail from Danai. Attached to the bear's mouth, she had inscribed a poem celebrating their love.

"Come with me." Daniel surprised Danai on her next exit weekend. He shoved two tickets to the famous Harare Under the Stars Theater into her palm. That evening, the couple joined other guests seated on the grass at Greenwood Park. Beneath sparkling stars and the brilliant moonlight, they held hands and watched lively Shona plays. When the performance ended, they danced in the wind and engraved their names on a hundred-year-old oak tree. They were Daniel and Danai, and there had never been anything like them.

"Daniel," Danai's voice screeched through the warm midday wind. "Daniel!"

"Do Danai's parents know their daughter's standing barefoot in broad daylight outside someone's gate screaming for some dude?" Daniel's brother teased. Daniel rose from the kitchen table and joined his brother at the window.

"Daniel, where are you? Come on, let's go." Clutching her pink sandals in one hand, she stood beneath an endless canopy of jacaranda trees. The blossoming purple trees filled every street in Harare and brilliantly hallmarked August, the month of Harare's Mega Show. Like the rest of the city, Daniel waited all year for this annual ten-day event. This year, he had made plans to go with Danai and her three unfriendly friends.

"Hurry, Daniel, let's go. I don't want to miss a thing." A breathless Danai barged into the kitchen. She abruptly stopped in her tracks. Her gaze shifted to Amai, who stood by the kitchen table next to Daniel.

"Come on, I'll drive you kids." Amai smiled, amused at Danai's meek greeting.

"We're here!" Daniel and Danai stared in awe at the vast landscape temporarily transformed into a massive entertainment and marketing city. Endless tents created the illusion of a vast silver sea, and a grand amusement park loomed on the horizon. Companies from every continent set up booths to display and launch their latest products.

"Are those your friends?" Amai pointed toward three girls waving in the distance.

"This is going to be the best show year ever!" Layla exclaimed as the couple approached the entrance. The group walked through the gates in time to catch a procession of fifty high school marching bands and their dancing majorettes. Danai and her friends frantically cheered for their emerald- and silver-wrapped school band.

"I'm feeling like art!" Sibo shouted. "The Warehouse, ladies?" She led the group to Mercedes Warehouse for Benz's yearly car show. This year, Mercedes had recruited ten up-and-coming young artists from ten countries around the world. Each artist had been assigned one car. The models ranged from a slick Mercedes 1957 SL Roadster to the recently launched CLK Convertible. Using bright paints and unique designs, each artist transformed their Benz into a moving canvas of art. Thembi Xhosa celebrated her Ndebele heritage by engaging in the traditional colorful geometric hut paintings. As the car gracefully made its way around the track, Daniel looked over at Danai. She looked mesmerized, stunned by the unconventional gallery of art-embedded cars.

"Maybe this will be you one day," he whispered to his entranced girlfriend, who nodded and wrapped her arm tightly around him. "That's my favorite." He pointed at German-Zambian painter Fitz's *Urban Graffiti*.

"Me too!" She laughed. The Mercedes show ended, and Daniel followed the girls through a growing crowd. The friends browsed stalls and purchased handcrafted earrings and intricately designed bracelets.

"Ladies, I'm getting hungry." Daniel groaned. "Let's check out Soweto Fifties." The girls nodded in agreement. Proudly celebrating Soweto 1950s street jazz culture, the venue was a marvel to anyone who stopped by. Large portraits of Hugh Masekela, Dorothy Masuka, and other famous African jazz singers clung to bare brick walls. During show week, the restaurant scheduled multiple live bands to play African jazz while patrons ate. Despite its unique ambiance, Soweto Fifties' greatest success lay in its eccentric menu. Each dish had a twist of southern African influence. Danai and her friends ordered mango-rooibos milkshakes with piri-piri fries and boerewors burgers. Daniel chose Kariba trout and roasted wild vegetables.

"It's time for evidence," Danai announced.

"Yes, it is," the girls said in unison.

"We do this every year," Thulani explained to Daniel.

The group left Soweto Fifties and made their way to a nearby T-shirt stall. Danai purchased five white T-shirts, and Layla paid to have each shirt spray-painted. In individualized script and coloring each shirt boldly declared, "Layla, Danai, Sibo, Daniel, and Thulani. Harare Show 1989."

"The two people who expect to have the most fun always buy the shirts and pay for the inscription," Thulani told Daniel. "It's evidence that this really happened." She giggled and put her T-shirt on over her outfit. Everyone followed suit, putting their T-shirts on.

"Come on, Daniel, you're a part of this. You have to join in." Layla motioned for him at the photo stand.

"Yes, Daniel, come on." The friends beckoned him. He joined the girls in front of the graffiti backdrop and posed for the evidence.

By evening, Daniel was exhausted but was enjoying hanging out with the girls. Danai's friends had become friendlier and were making a genuine effort to include him in their girls-only day.

"Safari Park, ladies," he suggested.

"Yes, of course," the girls shouted.

When they arrived, Safari Amusement Park was unexpectedly jam-packed. Daniel dragged Sibo and Danai to a shaking cheetah rollercoaster. The three braved the ride. After recovering, they joined Thulani and Layla on an enormous pink and blue Ferris wheel.

"Hey, it's already nine p.m." Sibo glanced at her watch. "If we go to KwaMombe, we can stand on the terrace and get a good view of the fireworks."

"Yeah, and you know everyone will be there," Layla added.

"Yes, they will." The other girls giggled in amusement.

Daniel discovered KwaMombe was a trendy restaurant bar situated at the edge of the show grounds. The "everybody" the girls claimed would be there was simply Sarchies' entire crowd—pretty girls, dealers, cliques, crews, and all. Cousin Arthur lazily sat at the bar with his latest girlfriend seated on his lap. From the restaurant's overcrowded terrace, Daniel looked down and stared in awe at thousands of people standing on grass, walkways, rooftops, and other terraces. The endless crowd gazed up at colorful fireworks illuminating the night sky. Daniel wrapped his arms tightly around Danai's waist and watched the blazing performance. Amid the blasts, he leaned over to Layla and said, "You were right! This is truly the best show year ever."

"Yes, it is. I told you so." Layla chuckled and pointed to her evidence.

Chapter Six
Superficial People

"Daniel."

"Yes, Amai."

"Have you met Danai's family yet?" Amai settled onto a chair at the kitchen table. "Her parents do know about you, right?"

"Yes, I think so." He didn't like the path this conversation was leading to. To deter her questions, he casually reached for a book on the joys of gardening. With feigned interest, Daniel breezed through its withered pages.

Amai's gaze remained locked on him. "Your father and I were talking last night. We both feel that Danai and you are spending a lot of time together. It's time we met her family. You know these things are important, Danny. Why don't you speak to her about it, son?"

"But Amai, it's not like Danai and I are planning on getting married," Daniel protested. "I mean, I'm seventeen and Danai's only fifteen!"

"I know, son, but its only when you meet a person's people that you begin to understand who they really are." She reached for a dishcloth and scrubbed the table. "Call Danai. I want to meet her family, okay, Danny?"

When he told her, Danai was less unenthusiastic than Daniel about Amai's proposal. However, she agreed to talk to her mother.

"It will be nice, son. You'll see," his mother insisted.

On Sunday afternoon Daniel's family left church and drove south of Harare's city limits. The Matambas lived in an emerging but hidden suburb. A unique neighborhood compromised of flourishing farms and large estates. Acres of crops organized into endless rows defined the vast landscape. Occasionally the thick green veil exposed a storied farmhouse or a beautiful mansion.

"There it is!" Daniel pointed toward a white structure on a hill. "Danai said we'd see a white house on the hill." Mr. Tashaya's Toyota Corolla ascended the winding road and drove through two towering marble pillars on either side of an electric gate.

"Danny, are you sure that Danai gave you the right address?" His mother's eyes danced in confusion. "This can't be someone's home, can it?"

The Toyota revved onto a circular mosaic courtyard. In the courtyard's center lay a gigantic water fountain surrounded by beds of green shrubbery. Sparkling water forcefully gushed out of the fountain's mouth, moistening the air before it whirled down and washed the ground. Islets of perfectly manicured glistening grass interrupted the courtyard's periphery. Each islet held an array of flowers: roses, lilies, carnations, and African daisies. One islet had been arranged to bloom shades of purple flowers, the next held an assortment of yellow flowers, and another islet had red flowers and another pink. The entire scene was breathtaking.

Daniel's father parked his Toyota between a beige Land Rover and a silver Mercedes Benz. The Tashayas stepped out of their vehicle and gasped in awe at a three-story ivory white structure resembling an elegant state house rather than a family home. Smooth pearl-white walls formed the mansion's three levels. Embedded in the geometric walls, gold arches framed large French windows. Delicate green vines coursed their way along four separate balconies, giving the entire structure a softer appearance. The Matambas' residence fully captured the opulence and splendor of Nouveau Afrique.

"Ah, kwazwai. Welcome!" A short, pudgy man appeared at the main entrance. Despite the smoldering heat wave, the man wore a suede smoking jacket, black pants, and a pair of gray sandals. "I saw you coming up the driveway. I'm Stan Matamba, Danai's father. Welcome to our humble abode." The man enthusiastically beckoned the guests.

Daniel grinned. Evidently Danai had inherited her looks from her father. Danai's father had the exact same smile and eyes as his daughter. They both shared a cinnamon complexion. Mr. Matamba, however, was an inch shorter and a hundred pounds heavier than his daughter.

"I think we just stepped into an episode of *The Rich and the Famous!*" Daniel's brother whispered to Daniel, staring at the white marble tiles. The two boys followed their parents into the Matambas' home.

"This is Mai Danai." Stan Matamba introduced his wife. Dressed in a flowing lavender dress and golden sandals, Mrs. Matamba stood gracefully next to a white suede sofa. Her tall, slender form sharply contrasted Mr. Matamba's round frame. With flawless ebony skin, beautifully defined facial features, and a captivating smile, the woman was simply stunning.

"And this is Mbuya." Mr. Matamba beamed as he introduced his aging mother. Wrapped in a thick blanket and tight traditional head wrap, the small woman sat on a separate white sofa. Despite her frail appearance, Mbuya Matamba's sharp eyes darted between the guests. She motioned for everyone to sit down. Momentarily abandoning his introductions, Stan rushed to his mother's side and refilled her glass with a concoction of Lion beer and Coca-Cola.

"And that young man is my son, Miles." Mr. Matamba grinned proudly and pointed to the boy descending the winding gold-plated stairwell. In Miles, Mr. Matamba had completely recreated himself. Miles was the mirror image of his father. "He's ten years old now, but one day he'll be a man, and I can finally retire and leave all this in his capable hands," Mr. Matamba confidently asserted. Daniel glanced at Miles' syrup-stained pudgy fingers.

With the introductions completed, the Tashayas settled onto the suede sofas. Mr. Matamba poured himself a glass of Cognac and lit his cigar. Daniel's father politely declined the offer of a cigar or alcoholic beverage. In response, Mrs. Matamba glided toward a small table that held a delicate Japanese tea set. She poured tea and Mazowe orange juice for the guests.

"I am pleasantly surprised by your knowledge and insight of our country's social structures, Mr. Matamba," Daniel's father commented as the adults launched into an in-depth discussion on Zimbabwe's social climate.

"I'm a lawyer," Mr. Matamba responded. "I have the privilege of meeting people from all circles of life. Besides, our family is like all Zimbabwean families. We have relatives living in the rural areas, in high density areas, and in the suburbs. What we don't hear in our daily lives, we are able to see whenever we visit our relatives."

"Lunch is served." Mr. Chris, the family's chef and head housekeeper appeared. The cheerful chef greeted the guests and led the way to the dining room.

"So, Daniel, how is school? What form are you in?" Mr. Matamba asked. Despite the man's friendliness, his gaze held a glimmer of disapproval.

"I'm in lower six, sir," Daniel nervously answered.

"Oh good! Then you got through those dreaded O-level exams." Stan Matamba almost looked sincere. "So, then, you must be seventeen?"

Daniel nodded. He had the strange feeling the man already knew the answers to the questions he was asking.

"One more year of high school, hey!" Mr. Matamba refilled Mbuya's glass with Lion beer and Coca-Cola. "And what are your plans for the future?"

"I don't know yet." Warm sweat tickled down Daniel's back. This was how witnesses must feel in the courtroom.

"Are you considering university?"

"Mmm, I'm not sure."

"Daniel is young." Daniel's mother interrupted Mr. Matamba's interrogation. Her eyebrows furrowed at the way this man was scrutinizing her son. "I believe he still has time to make up his mind. He'll most likely take a year off to explore his options."

"Yes, yes, I see your point, Mrs. Tashaya. Yes, it is important to explore all options," Stan Matamba agreed. His eyes darted toward his daughter. However, the man appeared to concede as he cut into his steak and thoughtfully chewed in silence. "Two years ago, my wife and I flew to the United States for vacation with our kids."

Mr. Matamba lovingly smiled toward his wife. She, in turn, gave him a quick nod of approval.

"We visited Atlanta, Miami, and North Carolina. It was a wonderful vacation." Mr. Matamba stopped talking long enough to refill both his and Mbuya's drinks. "While we were in the USA, my wife and I felt it would be a good idea to look into future opportunities for Danai. I know she was only thirteen at the time, but Mr. and Mrs. Tashaya, time is an expensive commodity. Loss of time equates to loss of purpose." He chuckled at his own analogy.

Mr. Chris returned carrying a tray of fried artichokes and yellow sweet potatoes. He served each of the guests and then left the room.

Mr. Matamba's eyes darted back to his wife. "When we saw the University of North Carolina in Chapel Hill, we knew. That campus is truly outstanding, and Chapel Hill probably has the best professors and faculty in the world. It ranks highly among America's state universities. So, after finishing high school, the plan is that Danai will go to UNC Chapel Hill." With his point made, Mr. Matamba took another sip of his shiraz and quietly settled into the rest of his meal.

At the end of their luncheon, Mrs. Matamba led everyone back to the family lounge for a small buffet of tropical fruits and assorted desserts. Determined to settle his curiosity, Daniel's father asked, "Mr. Matamba, you have all this land. What do you grow?"

"Well, we used to farm tobacco, but that stopped when we found out that Danai was buying cigarettes and smoking in her bathroom." Mr. Matamba released an exaggerated sigh. The guests all turned and stared at Danai. She sat, motionless, with the same blank face she'd held all afternoon. Mr. Matamba lit another cigar while his mother whipped out her snuff box and indiscreetly inhaled its ground tobacco contents. "Now we grow acres and acres of corn and wheat. Willards buys our supply and makes Corn Curls and Honey Krunchies—you know, children's cereal." Mr. Matamba gave a curious glance. "So, Mr. Tashaya, you said you run a business, but you never told me about your company. What exactly do you do?"

Daniel's father adjusted his suit jacket and announced, "I'm Senior Pastor of the African Methodist Episcopal church."

Mr. Matamba choked in surprise. "My daughter said you were into business, but she never mentioned that you are a man of the cloth." He shot an accusatory look toward his daughter. Daniel glanced over at Danai. She now held an amused smirk and was smiling for the first time since their arrival.

Mr. Tashaya noticed it, too. He momentarily assessed the fifteen-year-old, then turned his attention back to Mr. Matamba. "Mr. Matamba, God's business is real business. I oversee over one hundred and twenty churches throughout Africa, southeast Asia, and parts of western Europe."

From the periphery, Mbuya attempted to hide her snuff box, while Mr. Matamba quickly doused his cigar and shouted for Mr. Chris to come and remove the half-finished glasses of Cognac and Lion beer. For the remainder of the afternoon, Mr. Matamba and his mother listened soberly as Daniel's father discussed the administrative and business side of church ministry.

"And your goal?" Mr. Matamba inquired with genuine interest.

"To empower our people spiritually, mentally, physically, and even financially in God, of course. And ultimately progress Africa as a whole, with the church taking the lead, to become a more economically viable and responsible entity," Mr. Tashaya concluded, and Mr. Matamba nodded with new understanding.

When their visit ended, the Tashayas graciously thanked Danai's family for their hospitality. In return, the Matambas made Daniel's family promise to return for another visit. The blue Corolla hadn't driven far when Daniel's father stopped the car, and his parents burst into laughter.

"That house really is beautiful. It's like paradise, and all that land," Daniel's mother chanted. "But Daniel, what was your girlfriend wearing? I think that was inappropriate considering our visit." An image of Danai in her pink floral shorts and a halter top flickered through Mrs. Tashaya's mind. "You and Danai seem so different."

Daniel's father looked over from the steering wheel and smiled. "No, I like her. That girl is something else!" He chuckled and restarted the car, "Yes, I like Danai. Invite her to our home sometime for dinner." The Tashayas settled into a comfortable silence and drove into the sunset back to their home.

Chapter Seven
When Love Cries

Daniel staggered and landed face down in a pile of leaves. Reorienting himself, he rose back to his feet and squinted at his cousin, who looked unscathed. He shoved Arthur a second time, but Arthur swung, knocking him back into the bed of leaves.

"You're lying," Daniel screeched, but he knew Arthur never lied to him.

"Ask your boy, Jimmy. He was there, too. He saw it."

"You're lying because you're jealous. You're angry that I'm happy." Daniel wiped the blood trickling down his cheek. Clutching the tree trunk, he pulled himself back up.

"Whatever, man!" Arthur spat and wiped the dust off his shirt. "You need to check your girl. While you were sleeping, she was playing. Wake up, man." Without a second glance, he pushed open the rusty pink gate and left.

Paralyzed by the information Arthur had revealed, Daniel lay in bed for three days. He and Arthur had never fought, and Daniel didn't know how to digest his cousin's words or the fight in the aftermath.

Fearing the worst, Mrs. Tashaya called in a retired physician who lived three houses down.

"Mild dehydration due to profound shock," the doctor said. He left after giving Amai a recipe for a sugar and salt concoction.

On the fourth day, Daniel rose from his bed. After gulping down the ghastly concoction and taking a much-needed bath, he rushed out of his home. Arthur claimed that Jimmy had seen it, too, and Daniel was determined to find out the truth.

He found Jimmy at Belvedere Recreational Center playing basketball with the neighborhood boys.

"Hey, where have you been? I've been calling your house for days." His friend's gaze trailed from Daniel's face to the wrinkled garb Daniel wore. "Your mother said you were in bed, something about dehydration or something." Jimmy shook his head in amusement.

Jimmy had been Daniel's best friend for as long as Daniel could remember. They'd met shortly after Zimbabwe's independence when the Tashayas became the first Black family to move into Belvedere's segregated suburb. Jimmy broke the neighborhood's unspoken rule of separation when he approached Daniel and invited him to a game of pinball. Thus, Jimmy had become Daniel's first friend and only white friend. Fearing racial backlash, Mr. and Mrs. Tashaya initially refused to allow the boys to roam the neighborhood, but Jimmy kept coming to their home and inviting Daniel to hang out. Jimmy was the only white boy who could dance better than MC Hammer, and as the neighborhood became more integrated that talent made him popular in every circle.

A few months into their friendship, Jimmy had invited Daniel for dinner at his home. "The green house at the end of street." He grinned.

Daniel arrived carrying a bag of Granny Smith apples his mother had forced him to bring as a gift for Jimmy's mum. He entered the main gate and stood with his mouth opened wide on the porch as Jimmy proudly introduced his parents. Mr. and Mrs. Lee were both Black Zimbabweans, and no one offered any explanation. For the first time in his life, Daniel ate an entire meal in silence. Eight years of friendship and Jimmy never explained why this strange fact existed, so Daniel didn't ask

"I'm good." Daniel walked onto the court. He glanced at the other boys and shifted uncomfortably. They were watching the two friends with unusual interest. "Just needed to talk to you about something."

"Oh, here comes Kat. I wonder if he passed his O-levels this year," one of the neighborhood boys shouted, throwing the ball to Daniel. The remaining boys stopped playing and turned to stare at a boy stepping out of the passenger seat of a BMW. A muffled grumbling emanated throughout the court. With his signature permed afro and the three chains around his neck glittering in tarnished cubic zirconia, Kat slowly meandered onto the basketball court until he stood in Daniel's path.

They called him Kat because of the way he walked—stealthily with one foot steadily crossing over the other. This year marked Kat's fifth year taking the O-level exams, officially making him the oldest guy in high school. With each failure, he showed up at a different high school the following year. His parents saved face by paying a small sum each year to have him "transferred" rather than expelled. Behind Kat stood his boy, dubbed by the neighborhood kids as the Inmate because he looked like he'd become one someday.

"How is your girl, man?" Kat's sly eyes danced in contempt. His lips twisting in a way that made Daniel uneasy.

"My girl's good," Daniel emphasized. His eyes shot to the Inmate fidgeting in the background.

"You climbed a really high tree, but I recently heard a strange rumor." Kat grimaced, his eyes scanning the court to ensure that the observers were listening to his story.

"What did you hear, Kat?" the Inmate called from behind him.

"You climbed a really high tree, but I heard that branch broke." Kat cackled like he'd discovered an invaluable secret. The cubic zirconia chains around his neck jiggled haphazardly. "Maybe you should step aside and let real men like myself groom that tree."

"Like you said, that tree is already grown and budded." Daniel's lips quivered. He glanced at Jimmy, who held a serious expression and had moved closer to his side, "And some trees are too high for just any loser to climb."

"What?" Kat lunged forward, and the Inmate stepped in to hold him back. "You're lucky my boy's holding me back. I would have wiped this court with your face."

44

"You ain't wiping nothing with anything." Daniel smiled to hide the anger brewing within him. "Like I said, some trees are too high for the likes of you to climb. Man, my girl doesn't even know you exist." Daniel threw the ball back to a neighborhood kid and walked away.

"You okay?" Jimmy followed Daniel off the court. "Don't even entertain that nonsense." They walked farther from the crowd gathering on the court.

"Hey, Danny." Jimmy glanced back at Kat shouting obscenities in the distance, "Do you think Kat finally passed his O-levels this year?"

Daniel turned and stared at the blank expression on his friend's face. Both boys erupted into a fit of laughter until Jimmy fell rolling on the grass and Daniel felt like his insides were bursting out.

"Danny, you have to stop listening to everyone else's opinion." Jimmy lay on the grass attempting to catch his breath. "Danai's your girl. You trust her, right?"

From his position sitting at the edge of the tar road, Daniel nodded. With a serious expression, Jimmy sat up and calmly retold the events he'd witnessed at a party the weekend before.

"Go talk to her and find out what happened, okay?" Jimmy rose to his feet and hoisted Daniel from the ground.

"I have to go somewhere first," Daniel shouted. He ran down the street onto a main road to catch a minivan.

Flustered with confusion, Daniel paid the conductor and climbed out of the crowded minivan. The pungent scent of sweat and roasting pig feet trotters overwhelmed his senses. He entered Mbare Musika and surveyed the familiar marketplace. His life had been altered, yet the bustling marketplace remained unchanged. He walked past a cluster of women selling vegetables and used furniture.

"Come get them now—you know they'll be gone tomorrow." A man flaunted his updated line of BeatBoxes.

Daniel moved swiftly, avoiding the shrewd vendors and luring food stalls, until he arrived at Alice's Shabeen. Mai Chenai stood on a small ledge stirring a large pot of chicken gizzard stew. Three small boys played in the yard, running circles around an elderly man who leaned on his walking stick. The place looked desolate.

"Where's everyone?" Daniel walked into Alice's Shabeen.

Mai Chenai glanced at her watch and grinned. "They're coming." She wiped her soot-stained hands on her apron. As she descended from her ledge, a man in navy-blue overalls strolled in. The man turned to greet a group of women trailing in behind him.

"They're here!" Mai Chenai chuckled. The man in the navy-blue overalls flopped onto a crate and removed his gum boots. He sighed loudly and explained he'd worked the night shift at Woolworths Trading Company. Within minutes, a hungry crowd emerged and occupied the shabeen's thirty crates. Daniel grabbed a ginger ale and settled onto a broken chair near the hut's entrance. He listened quietly while customers and bystanders delved into stories they'd read in yesterday's newspaper. Once the crowd had exhausted each article, they ate in silence.

"I met a girl who dances like the wind." Daniel swallowed his pain and rose up. Ignoring the ache creeping through his belly, he stood among the crates. "Before I first met her, I already loved her." The crowd hummed in anticipation, and Mai Chenai handed him a second ginger ale. Daniel spoke, spilling the tale of his life and the girl who'd entered it. When he finished his story, he felt strangely empty and alone. He paid for his soda and left Alice's Shabeen.

"Why did I come to Mbare Musika?" he muttered as he moved through the crowd back to the taxi depot.

"Hey, little brother," a woman hollered from the distance, "Little brother, wait!" Glistening in fresh sweat and the curl activator dripping from her Jheri curls, the woman ran up to him. "I knew it was you." She wiped her hands on her floral dress and forcefully shook Daniel's hand. He politely pulled his hand away.

"Oh, you don't remember me?" The woman smiled broadly, revealing her missing tooth.

"The woman who married for love?" Daniel exclaimed, noting her freshly ironed floral dress and colorfully embroidered slippers. "What happened to you? You look happy!"

The woman's laughter caused bystanders to pause and pay attention. "Yes, that's me. How are you, little brother? Come and have a seat." She grabbed his arm and led him to a stall. Daniel wasn't sure why he followed her or sat on the barrel beside the stall.

"After I told my story that day, I felt so despondent. I decided to take my children and run away back to my parents' village." Her voice trailed off, and she reached to pick up a falling tablecloth. She hung it back on a washer line next to the stall before continuing her story. "So, I quit my job and left my boss's house. I carried away my few belongings, the crocheted tablecloths, and the curtains I knitted for comfort during my lonely nights working as a housemaid. You understand?"

47

Daniel slowly nodded, watching the curl activator dripping from the woman's curls.

"I had worked in that house for twelve years." Sadness filled her eyes. "That day, I stood at the bus stop by Avondale shopping center for over an hour, waiting for a minivan. Can you believe that it began raining? The rain was pouring so hard that everything I had was thoroughly soaked." The woman settled on a barrel next to Daniel's.

"When the rain stopped, I emptied my bag and spread the crocheted tablecloths and curtains on the grass to dry. A white woman walking her dog stopped in her tracks. She asked how much I wanted for the tablecloth. 'It's not for sale. I made it for my dream home,' I tried to explain, but the woman became infuriated. She shouted, 'I'll give you fifty dollars for the tablecloth and another fifty for the bedcovering and curtains, too.'"

"What?" Daniel gulped in astonishment.

"Yes, little brother. I made in that one day the same as my monthly wages working as a housemaid." The woman chuckled in glee. Spurts of curl activator danced on her head.

"I arrived at the shack that my husband and I lived in with his new wife and hid the money under a mulberry tree. Little brother, while the world laughed at my plight and my husband publicly ridiculed me, I sat in that shack and crocheted quietly. A month later, I packed my belongings and left with my four daughters. We now rent a small room in Kambuzuma, and I have my own stall!" She confidently waved her finger to the stall next to the barrel. Daniel's eyes widened. Adjacent to the stall, rows of intricately crocheted pearl white tablecloths, bed coverings, and curtains hung on washer lines. Beams of sunlight seeped through delicate loops creating clusters of dancing kaleidoscopes. The breathtaking creations swayed gracefully in the noon breeze.

"Little brother, can you believe—after I left my husband, I became my own boss." Her laughter soaked the atmosphere. "I now make enough money to send my girls to good schools. In a few months, I'll have enough to purchase my own home."

Moving from the stall's shade, the woman hurried to catch a falling bed covering. Under the sunlight, the glimmering sweat and curl activator created a subtle hue causing her to shine brilliantly while she stood next to her premium handmade products. Daniel noticed a soft dimple in her cheek and smiled.

"You've done well, big sister," he exclaimed.

"Yes, I know." She glowed radiantly. "Go home, little brother. You're going to be alright."

Daniel unlatched the rusty pink gate and strolled through the yard. Freshly washed laundry hung outside the kitchen entrance. The familiar scent of lemon floor polish filled his nostrils. Amai sat near a window chopping pumpkin leaves. She looked lost in her thoughts.

"Good afternoon, Amai." He walked into the kitchen.

"Aah, you're back! Where did you run out to?" She set aside the mass of green leaves and poured him a glass of Mazowe orange juice. "How are you feeling?" He'd missed this, the comfortable feeling of his mother's presence.

"Arthur came by earlier. He wanted to check on you." Amai reached onto the kitchen counter and handed him an envelope. "He left this for you."

49

Daniel opened the envelope and pulled out a ticket to Dynamos soccer team's semifinal game. On the back of the ticket, Arthur had inscribed: "It's your favorite soccer team. Hope I'll see you there, cousin."

"What happened? Did you two fight?"

"No, Amai." Daniel smiled at his mother.

"You look tired, and you haven't eaten in three days." She scooped warm goat meat stew into a bowl and placed it on the table. "What is wrong, my son? Did something happen?" Amai settled back into her seat at the kitchen table.

Daniel bent over and unzipped his knapsack. He pulled out a crocheted tablecloth and handed it to his mother.

"What is this, Danny?" Amai slowly trailed her fingers though the delicate pearl white loops. "It's exquisite, Danny. Where did you get this? Who made it?"

"I bought it from a woman who married for love." Daniel settled at the table next to Amai. He picked up a kitchen towel and wiped the dust off his face and hands. With great effort, he shoved the first spoonful of goat meat stew into his mouth. Chewing thoughtfully, he ate until the bowl was empty.

"Amai," Daniel said and swallowed the final spoonful. With sadness, he looked up at his mother and told her, "Danai cheated on me."

Chapter Eight
Suspicious—Danai's Confession

"I didn't cheat." Danai wept as she waded through the furious wind. Tears streamed down her cheeks. Her foot plunged into an overripe rotting mango scattered along the roadside, causing her to slide and stumble. She looked up to see Daniel's mother shaking her head in the distance. In that moment, both Daniel's home and Mrs. Tashaya seemed unfamiliar. With disappointment on her face, Daniel's mother walked back into the house and swung the door shut.

"I didn't cheat," Danai muttered to the isolated road. "Not really."

Her legs spontaneously moved while her mind wandered back to events two weeks earlier. Had it only been fourteen days ago when she and Layla sat in Ricky's Ice Cream Shack?

"Danai, this is boring and I'm tired. I'm going home, girl." Layla had risen from her seat.

"I'm going to Lillian's house," Danai had announced, feeling annoyed.

"Who?" Layla had asked in confusion.

"Lillian, my mother's youngest sister. You know, the one who lives in Avondale." Danai had noted her friend's concerned expression. "You remember my aunt Lilly. She used to model for Petite-Size Warehouse and now works as an air hostess for Air Zimbabwe."

"Danai, it's getting late. I really think we should both just go home," Layla had insisted.

Danai had rejected her friend's advice then, but today, as she waded through rotting mangos, she wished she had listened to Layla. A minivan speeding in her direction honked angrily, jerking Danai out of her thoughts. In her haste to retreat, she lost her balance and landed on the mushy earth. *Had Daniel's mother witnessed this second fall?* Danai lifted her head, her eyes instinctively searching the empty porch in the distance.

The yellow minivan stopped. "Ah, sisi, sorry, I didn't see you there," said the driver. "Do you need a ride? I'm heading to the city." Ignoring her muddy appearance and the pungent smell of rotting fruit, he allowed the broken girl to enter his yellow van. She settled in the seat behind the driver. As the van turned the corner, Danai glanced back at Daniel's house.

"He's not here," Mrs. Tashaya had triumphantly stated earlier that day. She'd opened the door just wide enough to assess Danai, then gasped at how distraught the girl appeared. "Like I told you last time, he's not here." The woman recovered her cold demeanor. A curtain at a side window swayed, stealing both Danai and Mrs. Tashaya's attention. Quick footsteps hurried away.

"Danai, you've come here three times already. Don't you think this is a little too much, even for you?" Mrs. Tashaya had ignored the moving curtain. "Danai?"

"Yes, Amai."

"Amai!" The woman had laughed haughtily. "Amai! How am I your mother? I just asked you a question. Don't you think this is a little too much?"

"I'm sorry, Amai," Danai had mumbled.

"Go home," Mrs. Tashaya had turned her back on the weeping girl. "And don't ever come back again."

The yellow van stopped at an intersection. Exhausted, Danai rested her face on the cold window and closed her eyes. Memories of her visit to Lillian's home two weeks earlier filled her thoughts. Danai remembered entering the warmth of her aunt's lounge.

"I'm not sleeping." Lilly's voice echoed from the bedroom. "I'm too jetlagged to sleep. That Paris-to-Harare flight is no joke. It really got me, plus we had one of those demanding passengers. Another drink, another blanket." Sounds of laughter poured out of the television set.

"Danai, where are you? I bought you something." Danai heard the sound of ruffling paper and then Lilly's soft footsteps. "Oh, there you are. Here take this." Lillian came into the lounge and handed Danai a colorful duty-free shopping bag. "Where's Layla? Didn't you say you guys were coming together?"

"She changed her mind." Danai frowned. "She said she wanted to go home."

"Really." Lillian handed Danai a second gift bag. "This one's for your mother. I already called your baba and asked if you could spend the night here." The youngest of Mrs. Matamba's sisters, Lilly's personal philosophy at twenty-one was simply "life is now." Lilly reached back into her suitcase and pulled out a short black velvet dress and a pair of green rhinestone stilettos. "Get ready, Danai. We're going out."

"What? Where are we going? I didn't bring anything to wear," Danai protested. Her aunt walked to her bedroom closet and pulled out an old pair of jeans and a vibrant viscose shirt.

"They're Charlie's." She giggled and reached for a razor to slice horizontal layers through the jeans, creating the fashionable ripped jeans look.

Danai put on the jeans and tied the red viscose shirt at her waist.

"Wow, you look good! Charlie's going to be so mad, but I warned him to stop leaving his stuff at my house." Lillian laughed as she imagined her younger brother's reaction. "Hey, I heard that Daniel's family came to visit your home last month. Is that true?"

"Yeah, they did."

"Really. Where was I? What did Babamukuru do? Did he bring up UNC Chapel Hill?" Lilly chuckled at the thought of her brother-in-law. "Well, you and Daniel are still together, so it couldn't have gone too badly, right?"

It began with a sound—the doorbell rang. Danai didn't hear it, but Lillian did. Her aunt rushed out of the bedroom into the living room.

She opened the door and embraced her boyfriend, Godfrey. Godfrey kissed Lilly and entered the house. Known as the forever couple, Godfrey and Lillian had been together for as long as anyone could remember. At five foot two with dark chocolate skin, full lips, and almond shaped eyes, Lillian resembled a pretty doll. Godfrey, on the other hand, was tall and stout. An unruly mass of curly blond hair contrasting his bronze skin revealed his mixed heritage. Together, the couple looked beautiful. At eighteen, Godfrey had signed on with an overseas soccer team. In so doing, he'd transformed his talent for soccer into a lucrative business. He walked out of high school with his high school diploma and a seven-figure contract. Now at nineteen, he was living the life of his dreams.

The grinning Godfrey walked into the room with three tall boys trailing behind him. Dressed in pleated pants, shiny shoes, and trendy cropped jackets, the boys resembled a boy band.

"The Richlorne Crew!" Danai whispered to herself. Nyika Tumai, Derek Love, and Makhosini Moyo. Will B., the fourth member, was notably absent. She'd seen the crew before but always from a distance. Today, standing near the kitchen entrance, Danai stared in awe. They were all around six feet tall and handsome with smooth charcoal black skin. Their very presence demanded attention.

The boys strolled into the room and settled onto the couch. Lilly sat next to Godfrey and retold the story of her stopover at Heathrow Airport and the unruly passenger.

"How old are you?" Nyika glanced toward the kitchen. A subtle dimple appeared in Nyika's left cheek as he spoke. With unabashed curiosity, he stared at the girl standing by the doorway as if noticing her for the first time.

"Sixteen," Danai lied.

"Really?" Nyika's eyes flickered in amusement before he playfully winked at Derek Love.

"You can't lie to Nyika." Derek laughed. "Nyika knows everything about the ladies."

"Yes, I do, 'cause the ladies love Nyika T!" The two boys locked hands and engaged in an elaborate handshake while Godfrey and Makhosini Moyo laughed.

"That's Danai, my niece." Lillian's stern tone interrupted the boys' mischief. "Guys, stop playing around and lets go."

The boys obediently followed Lilly out of the house and crammed into Godfrey's Mazda 626.

"Where is this party?" Nyika attempted to stretch his legs in the backseat.

"Right here," Godfrey answered as he parked his Mazda. A forbidding white wall greeted guests. Two guards stood outside the electric gate inspecting each invitation.

"She's with me." Nyika grabbed Danai's hand to deter the guard from scrutinizing her. The gate opened and the group gasped at the sight of a beautiful Grecian-style mansion.

"Hey, you're on your own." Nyika released Danai's arm and rushed off into the crowd. Lillian and Godfrey headed in the opposite direction. Danai walked further in and surveyed her surroundings. The mansion's large backyard had been converted into a party island with a full bar and bartender. Amid the yard, a makeshift wooden dance floor easily supported the hundred people clamoring on it. DJ Tonite grinned as he stood behind his turntables. At the far end of the yard lay a large rock quarry softened by a waterfall. The quarry's waters flowed down the rocks into a swimming pool, and a romantic Japanese bridge arched from one end of the pool to the other. Mesmerized, Danai settled onto a garden chair next to Makhosini Moyo and Derek Love.

"What does he do?" Derek asked.

"Who knows?" Makhosini raised his eyebrows. "Apparently no one knows." Both boys looked up and suspiciously assessed the mansion owner. He seemed to be in his early thirties. The reticent man had appeared six months ago from nowhere and somehow penetrated their exclusive society.

Danai's gaze followed the direction the boys were looking. In the distance, Rumbi, Harare's top model, clung onto her infamous boyfriend, businessman James Tendayi. The two stood among a group of glamorous-looking people that Danai had only seen in Drum magazine.

"Well, if I'm going to get my woman back, I better go find out what James Tendayi does, right?" Derek chuckled. He rose from his seat and headed toward the group.

"So, what do you think about your first Dhindindi?" Makhosini turned to the girl seated next to him.

"I like." Danai echoed Guy's hit song, laughing.

"It's not Sarchies—no youngsters here. Well, almost." He smiled.

"What, me?" Danai feigned surprise. "Most of the people here are only two, maybe three years older than me. Like you, you're probably seventeen or eighteen."

"You're right, I am." He gave her a brotherly smile. "However, most of the people here are twenty, twenty-one, and even twenty-five."

"Oh!"

"Yes, Danai," Makhosini mused. "Don't rush life, Little Girl. This is 'all that glitters,' but it's not all gold." He leaned back, rested his head on the garden chair and closed his eyes. "By the way, you look nice tonight."

"Thank you. You look nice, too."

"Ah, Makhosini, you're here!" A thick-bodied girl in a yellow body-hugging dress leaned over the table. "And who is this? Did you bring your little sister?"

"This is whoever she wants to be," Makhosini lazily responded.

"Does 'whoever she wants to be' have a name?"

"If she's old enough to be here, she's old enough to tell you her own name."

Leaning toward Danai, the yellow dress owner announced, "I'm Helene, and you are?"

"I'm the little sister," Danai blurted and turned her attention back to the dance floor.

Helene's eyes darted to the boy slouched with closed eyes. "Makhosini, when you're ready to deal with a real woman, call me. I'll be waiting. And next time, why don't you leave your *little sister* at home?"

"Are you hungry?" Makhosini rose from his seat.

"What?" Danai stared at him.

"I'm going to get something to eat. Does my little sister want anything?" He grinned. A rush of fury swept through Helene's eyes

58

before she disappeared into the growing crowd. Makhosini strolled to the kitchen and returned, carrying a plate stacked with chicken wings and a cherry plum for Danai.

"Ooh, I love this song." Danai rose from her seat. With her arms stretched upward, she swayed to the music. Amused, Makhosini laughed and covered his eyes with one hand.

"Every time I see you, you're dancing." He uncovered his eyes and watched her playfully tapping her feet. "Do you like it that much?"

Danai looked up. The crowd appeared to be pulsating to the beat of the music. "When I'm dancing, everything around me disappears." Her eyes danced with the music. "The people, even things I worry about, nothing matters any more. It's just me and the music. I feel free, like I'm floating." She moved her arms in a wave-like motion and glanced at Makhosini. Surprisingly, he had stopped laughing and was watching her intently.

"I guess it's like when I'm racing my bike," he whispered into her ear. "At that moment, I feel the wind rushing through my body, and I know I can make it through anything."

"I think you need to dance." Danai burst into laughter. Entranced, Makhosini watched the girl moving to the pulse of everything around them.

"What's it like?" Danai watched Makhosini chew on his last chicken wing.

"What is what like?" he asked.

"People treat you like you're what glitters." She giggled at her own analogy. "It's almost like everything waits for you and nothing starts without you."

Makhosini stared at her. Deliberately avoiding his gaze, Danai laughed. Makhosini leaned back into the garden chair and closed his eyes.

"Tell me what's it like," Danai mumbled into the night air. "How does it feel?"

Makhosini's eyes opened just wide enough for him to see the world he was sitting in. His gaze purposely trailed from Danai's eyes, down to the edge of her mouth before settling on her trembling hands. Staring back into her eyes, he placed a feather-soft kiss on her lips. Danai gasped in surprise. The distinct taste of fresh mint and honey teased her senses. Makhosini's kiss enticed and beckoned her to follow him. His lips whispered into Danai's soul then ignited heaven. This kiss reached into her dreams, exposing her silent fears intermingled with Makhosini's hidden loneliness.

"It feels like this," he whispered.

Frantically pulling away, Danai looked up. The crowd appeared frozen. Everyone stood, staring at her and Makhosini. Alarmed at the unwarranted attention, she pushed Makhosini away. DJ Tonite stared up in confusion. Turning up his amp, he blasted Bell Biv DeVoe's "Poison," and the wave of silence dismantled.

"And it feels like that." Makhosini watched the onlookers slowly turn to cheer a white boy who danced like MC Hammer. Leaning back into the garden chair, he closed his eyes. He'd felt it too. Something deep in his soul ignited. Like the wings of butterflies, it playfully fluttered without restraint into his being.

From her periphery, Danai saw her aunt emerge from the dance floor. Lillian released Godfrey's hand and pushed her way through the crowd. Without hesitation, she yanked Danai out of her seat.

"Are you crazy, Makhosini? Have you lost your mind?" Lilly demanded in a barely audible voice. "I don't piss in your garden, so don't play in my house." Without another word, Lillian dragged her niece toward the electric gates.

"I'm not playing or pissing!" Danai heard Makhosini's voice behind her.

"Sisi, sisi, wake up!" a male voice commanded. Danai abruptly woke up. Her face winced at the coldness of the van window. The nauseating smell of rotting mangos filled her nostrils. "Where am I?" she mumbled, wiping drool off her cheek and brushing her mud-caked dress. Her eyes opened wide as she stared at the familiar marble courtyard and her mother's Land Rover.

"You're home, sisi," the driver replied. His kind eyes calmed her anxiety. She remembered him and his yellow minivan. Earlier, he'd offered her a ride on the deserted street outside Daniel's home. She winced at the memory of the moving curtain and the look of disappointment on Mrs. Tashaya's face.

"You looked like you needed some help, so I drove you home," the fatherly driver explained. "You said this was your address, right?" He reached back and opened her door. Fresh tears filled Danai's eyes and trickled down her face.

"Thank you," the broken girl whispered. She stepped out of the yellow van. Ignoring the freezing rain, Danai walked slowly through the courtyard. Slouching down on the cold marble pavement between blossoming tulips and weeping willows, she wept.

Dear Daniel,

How are you? I'm not doing so good. I tried calling you lots of times. Every time your brother answered and said you were too busy to speak to me. So, today I went to your house. Your mother told me to leave and never come back again. But how can I not come back to you, Danny? Please ask me what really happened, ask me if I cheated on you. I miss you, Danny, and I'm still here sitting in the rain—waiting for you.

Love,

Danai

Chapter Nine
Where Do We Go From Here?

"Ah, girls, did you hear the latest news?" A girl ran into Wimpy Burger Hut, breathless. Her high heels pounded the peeling tile floor, causing patrons to lift their heads and stare. Her haphazard knot of braids bounced to the excited thump of her heels. She rushed toward four girls gathered at a corner table.

"What news? What happened, Helene?" her friends responded.

Hurrying, the girl collided with a waiter and screeched. Ignoring the startled waiter and the curious observers, she righted herself and darted toward her friends.

"Melissa's crying!" she bellowed.

"What? Why? When?" her friends shouted.

"Melissa found out!" The girl's lips overflowed with malice. "She found out and cried for days. I mean, wouldn't you? I told you that everyone saw him kiss that girl."

"Makhosini could have any girl. I wonder what he was doing with that girl," another girl blurted in disbelief.

"Who was she anyway? Do we know her?"

"Just some little girl. She's sort of pretty." Helene leaned on the table and described the girl she'd seen with Makhosini at a party three weeks earlier. "Unusual looking with big lips, big hips, crazy outfit. A beautiful body and an ugly attitude!" Reaching for a glass on the table, she gulped down its icy contents and vigorously wiped the drips from the side of her mouth. Her clan scooted their chairs to make room for their unruly leader. As if guessing her friends' next question, the girl eagerly continued, "He told her. He called Melissa the next day and told her. After two years together, he does something this stupid."

"Well, good for us," one of her friends cackled. "Makhosini is finally single and free!"

The girls broke into a frenzy of laughter.

"Not quite!" the pack's leader cautioned. "Makhosini and Melissa have decided to try and work it out, and apparently he is trying."

Her friends shook their heads and hummed their collective disappointment.

The air thickened as Danai struggled to breathe. Chocolate milkshake curdled down her throat. Initially, she'd listened passively, paying little attention to the girls' banter. As the conversation continued, she realized that *she* was the person the girls were discussing. Perplexed, she swiveled around. Her eyes searched the tables behind her. Five girls gathered around a corner table, engrossed in their tantalizing conversation. Helene sat at the far end of the table. She wore the same tight yellow dress she'd worn to the party three weeks earlier. Oblivious to Danai's presence and fueled by her friends' interest, Helene continued chewing her tasty morsel of gossip.

She sucked her breath in exaggerated exasperation. "To make matters worse, that little girl had a boyfriend. Yes, can you believe that?"

"Aah, what?" Her friends' voices resonated throughout the restaurant.

"Yes! Some boy from Sabersvale High. He's Arthur's cousin—can't remember his name though. Apparently, that boy found out, and he's up and left her."

"Eeh!" The girls shook in giggles.

"Yes, girls," Helene's face twitched with excitement. She glanced at the patrons who'd stopped eating to watch her. Her eyes danced at the unexpected attention. "Rumor has it that the weekend after everything happened, the boy went to a house party. He met some other girl. Now they are dating!"

"What?" The girls clasped their hands and laughed gleefully.

Dismayed, Danai's insides twisted.

Helene looked up and gasped when she locked eyes with Danai. She motioned for her friends to stop talking. Her clique turned and stared at the lone girl.

"His name is Daniel," Danai blurted. She slowly rose from her seat. "His name is Daniel." Surrendering, she scurried out of the restaurant.

Soaked in humiliation, Danai wandered aimlessly around the city for hours. She stumbled into a pay phone and dialed the number that felt like it had been engraved on her heart with her tears.

Daniel answered. The gentle sobbing of the girl he'd once opened his life to invaded his surroundings.

"Danai, is that you? Are you okay?"

"Why haven't you called me back?" she whispered between sobs. "I've called you lots of times."

"I've been busy, you know, with school and all," Daniel's uneasiness seeped through the telephone. "Where are you, Danai?"

"Is it true, Daniel? Did you go to a party and meet someone else? While I've been coming to your home begging your mother, have you been dating someone else?"

"Danai, we have visitors. I really can't talk right now."

"Just answer me, yes or no," she screeched, but she already knew the answer.

"Yes, it's true. I met someone new, and yes, I'm dating someone else," Daniel's words spilled out like water on flames of fire.

Danai stopped crying and wiped the remaining tears from her face. Sobered with reality, she hung up the phone and walked out of the phone booth.

Chapter Ten
Family Intervention

Danai's six-week school break began, but she remained shrouded in the solitude of her room, hidden from the rest of world. Melodies of singers who'd apparently suffered significant heartbreak emanated from her hiding place, filling the house.

Frustrated at the unwelcome disruption of their family's harmony, Mr. and Mrs. Matamba intervened. Baba barged into Danai's room one evening.

"You know, sometimes I look at you and think of my father." He sat on the bed next to his daughter. "Maybe it's because you look so much like him."

"What was he like?" Danai turned to her father.

"Sekuru was a quiet and discreet man. A man of few words and even fewer possessions but incredibly wise with great dreams." A visible warmth swept over Baba's face. "You know, he was a goat herder. A man who loved and protected his family ferociously. I remember when he heard about a missionary school offering free education for Black Zimbabweans. Sekuru packed me up and sent me there, to Makudzwa Mission."

"How old were you?" Curiosity lured Danai into Baba's story.

"Seven years old! Still a baby." Mr. Matamba shook his head. "Makudzwa Mission was an entire day's journey away. It was a difficult school. For years, I saw my family one weekend a month. I couldn't understand why, so I resented my father. I thought he sent me there to show off his educated son to the other villagers." Mr. Matamba looked to see if his daughter was still listening. Satisfied, he readjusted his jacket.

"You resented Sekuru?"

"Yes, I did." Baba chuckled at the memory of his father. "But as I grew older, I began discovering the man Sekuru was, and that's when I understood. My father simply wanted me to live the life he hadn't had. Not just an education or more possessions, but greater dreams. At that time, this country was locked in apartheid and its atrocities. The law was designed to keep Black people uneducated and poor. We even had to carry special pass cards just to visit our family in other villages. Those were very hard times. Sekuru wanted me to live the things he only dared to hope for."

Danai sat up and watched her father. Streaks of gray seeped through the tight coils on his head. Though he was smiling, her father looked tired. His eyes wandered around the room until his gaze settled back on his daughter.

"I look at you, Danai, and I see my hopes and dreams. The possibilities of everything you can be. You are special, very loved. And you know what? You come from a long line of people who've faced adversity and survived. You're going to be something great. Only you can take that from you. Do you understand?"

"I don't know." Danai wasn't sure if she understood.

"Things happen in life, but you have the power to make a choice to remain focused and not get caught up in all the confusion." Her father smiled wryly.

"But Baba, I feel so bad. I feel embarrassed." Her voice trailed off as she remembered the girls at Wimpy. "People are saying things about me, not nice things."

"That's life, Danai." Baba laughed. "Someone somewhere will always have something to say. You only have two questions to ask."

"What's that?"

"Are they feeding you—when you are hungry, do they feed you? And if you were sick, would they care for you or pay your hospital bills? If they are not contributing to your life, what right do they have to try to dictate your tomorrow?"

"But Baba, you don't understand," Danai mumbled.

"No, my daughter, I do understand." Baba gently patted her back.

"Baba." She watched her father's silhouette. "Daniel left me."

"Yes, I know." Mr. Matamba reached through the shadows and held his daughter's hand. Danai clung onto her father's hand and wished he would never let go.

The next day, Mrs. Matamba chose a different approach. She came home early. Her voice resonated throughout the house. "Danai, I think it's time you left this house. Your school break is almost over, and you and I need a makeover." Mrs. Matamba dragged her daughter toward the beige Land Rover. "And let's go get some food."

As they arrived, her mother whispered, "This is my favorite restaurant." They strolled into Jameson Hotel's Prestige Lounge. With only two other patrons, the room felt comfortably empty.

"Are you okay?" Mrs. Matamba settled into the seat opposite her daughter. "Danai, are you okay?"

Danai looked down and tugged at the hem of her skirt. "No, Mama, I'm not okay," she mumbled. Her eyes darted back up, searching her mother's face for disapproval. She saw none.

Mother and daughter sat in silence. In unison, they lifted their knives and began cutting into their steaks.

"You'll be alright," her mother decided. "Life is funny like that. You're walking on this path. Everything's clear, and then something unexpected happens and life takes an abrupt turn. Just when you think everything is falling apart, something new is forming. That's life, Danai."

"How do you know that I'll be okay?" Danai glanced at an elderly woman seated at the table next to theirs. The woman sipped on a glass of sherry and then went back to quietly knitting a sweater.

"I know because I am your mother and you're a part of me." Mrs. Matamba smiled. "You know, in life, sometimes you'll make the right choices. A lot of times we make mistakes and when you do, you simply learn from it and do better the next time."

"But I messed up," Danai confessed.

"Maybe you did, maybe you didn't." Her mother's tender gaze rested on her. "Either way, don't you think you've punished yourself enough?" Mother and daughter stared across the table, looking into one another. In unison, they lifted their knives and finished off their steaks.

"What's that?" Danai watched her mama pull out an elaborately wrapped box. Mrs. Matamba unwrapped the box and handed it to her daughter.

"Wow! A Kodak camera." Danai's eyes danced in appreciation. "Thank you, Mama. I've always wanted one."

"I hope in your journey through life, you'll take many photos. Learn from the bad and save the good." Mama laughed. "Give yourself room to breathe and fall. Then get up again, brush it off, and keep on moving."

The following afternoon, Danai joined her friends in the city. The girls rampaged through Ximex mall's endless stores while moaning about the woes of returning to boarding school.

"These breaks are too short," Sibo protested. "We should only go to school for six months, then relax and do what we want for the other six months."

"You know your mother would never let you relax." Thulani envisioned Sibo's overbearing mother and chuckled. As the girls moved from store to store, nobody asked about Daniel, but Danai was acutely aware of his absence.

"It was his loss," Layla whispered into Danai's ear. "But it's my gain. Now I can spend more time with my best friend." The two girls giggled and locked arms in the rebirth of their friendship.

71

Chapter Eleven
You and Me, This Song Called Us

"Our midterm break starts today," Danai pleaded over the school phone. "Can I spend the night at Auntie Lilly's? Please, Mama?"

"Biology, chemistry, art, mathematics." Danai heard Thulani reading out loud in the background. "Geography, physics, African history, Shona literature."

"It's crazy, right?" Sibo threw her clothes into her trunk, "Can you believe what we just went through for the last two months? I'm gonna tell my mother I'm done with high school."

"Yeah right." Thulani rolled her eyes.

"Danai, I don't think spending the night at Lillian's place is a good idea." Mrs. Matamba ignored the voices in the background. "Your break is only ten days long. We haven't seen you since the semester began. Besides, Mbuya and Baba have been waiting for you to come home."

"I know, Mama, but please can I spend tonight at Lilly's? I promise I'll come home tomorrow," she pleaded until her mother conceded.

"Aah, so they finally released you from the shackles of boarding school!" Lillian laughed at her niece's unexpected arrival.

"I thought you loved high school," Danai teased. She entered the warmth of her aunt's home.

"Wait till you start working. That's when you'll resent the clutches of higher education." Lilly stirred a pot of beef stew. "Girl, what's been going on? Why haven't I seen or heard from you in over three months?"

"I needed some time by myself." Danai chuckled. To her aunt's dismay, she stuck her thumb into the pot and licked the delicious sauce.

"For three months!" Lillian exclaimed. "And when are you going to learn to cook?"

"I don't have to learn because I'm planning on moving in with you." Danai giggled and wrapped her arms around her aunt, then sat at the kitchen table. "Lilly, why didn't you tell me Makhosini had a girlfriend called Melissa?"

"First of all, you and Makhosini didn't consult anyone before your little act." Lillian stopped chopping onions and stared at her niece. She opened the fridge and handed Danai a glass of Mazowe orange juice.

"Secondly, I didn't think you cared about the whole Makhosini situation. Why? What happened?"

Danai told her aunt about Helene and the girls at Wimpy Burger Hut.

"I'm sorry to hear that. I know you really liked Daniel." Lilly's sympathy filled the distance between them. "I didn't tell you about Melissa because the day after the party, Makhosini did tell her what happened, and they broke up. Things had been up and down with them for a while, and I guess that was the straw that broke the camel's back. Makhosini's been single for months." She placed a lid on the ceramic pot. "That Helene should mind her own business or get her stories straight. And she needs to invest in a new dress, one that fits!" Without another word, she picked up the remote and turned on the TV.

"So, I hope you brought your own clothes this time. 'Cause no staying at home tonight. And you can't slice or dice anything else in here. Charlie's still fuming about his favorite outfit." Lilly chuckled as she remembered her younger brother's reaction to his demolished jeans. To her amusement, Danai reached toward the floor and unzipped a large duffle bag. Layers of clothes fell out as the doorbell rang.

"Aah, guys, look at this." Derek walked in. "Our little girl has finally come out of hiding!" Draped in colorful suits and classic fedoras, the Richlorne crew trailed in behind Derek.

"Hey, she's all cried out fifteen." Nyika grinned and hoisted Danai up. "Now she really must be sixteen." The room erupted into laughter, and she blushed.

"Okay, my people," Nyika hollered. "Its's time to party!"

Known for its exotic Asian-African cuisine, Grace Silk Factory had recently opened its doors. A massive banner welcomed guests: "Happy Birthday Nyika." With the touch of balloons, streamers, and DJ Tonite on the turntables, the Silk Factory had been transformed into Nyika Tumai's personal party haven. Nyika reached into his pocket, pulled out a golden whistle, and forcefully blew to announce his own arrival.

Ladies lavishly wrapped in satin dresses and guys sporting trendy suits overflowed the colorful room. Danai was glad she had taken Lilly's advice on wearing the simple blue organza dress. People greeted each other as if they hadn't seen each other in years. The night's atmosphere was truly contagious. Rumor had it that some of Nyika's guests had flown in from Zambia, Johannesburg, and London.

Midnight struck. The music became barely audible as DJ Tonite's voice filled the room. "Ladies and gents, tonight I bring to you the man who begins it all, Mr. Nyika Tumai."

The crowd cleared the dance floor.

"La-la-ladies, he's eighteen now," Tonite announced. "He's getting old! You better catch him tonight." Dealers lit their lighters and lifted the dancing flames into the air. Men hollered and ladies clapped. Amid the cheers, Nyika made his way to the center of the dance floor and broke into a smooth running man. DJ Tonite released two seconds of MC Hammer's "Can't Touch This."

Nyika grabbed the mic and loudly cleared his throat. "Thank you, people, for coming to my humble shabeen. Every man has a crew, so allow me to introduce you to mine." His eyes swept over the crowd. "Ladies, he's a sweet smile, and gents, he's a right arm of steel. Lift it up for the man of love, Mr. Derek Love," Nyika chanted and glided into another running man.

The crowd exploded into frenzied applause.

"In the right corner, Godfrey, Zimbabwe's gorilla ball-spinner and our newest millionaire," Nyika declared as though millionaires were raining out of the sky. "At the gorilla's side is his forever wifey, the ever-beautiful, always-tasteful Auntie Lillian. You know her as our orchid of these streets." He grinned and laughed into the mic. Dealers released gangster whistles while thugs shouted homage.

"Ah ladies, the man of this and every hour, Zimbabwean-bred, Harare-grown, my best friend, the ever-chillin' Mr. Makhosini 'smooth-daddy' Moyo. It is always about you, man."

In response, Makhosini casually leaned onto the bar and broke into a quick smile. A mass hysteria of cheers erupted, and DJ Tonite released three more seconds of beats.

Just as Nyika appeared to wrap up his MC moment, he slid toward Danai. "Laaaadies and gents, how can we ever forget our famous Little Girl?" He grinned and the crowd roared. "Her name is Danai. We like her. And Little Girl, this world is yours." Nyika pulled Danai to the dance floor. They flowed into the cabbage patch dance. "Finally, my people, please lift it up for the ladies, 'cause laaaadies you always look so delicious. Let's party, Tonite!" Nyika shouted.

"Oh, Casanova!" DJ Tonite spun LeVert's hit melody, and a wave of guests rushed back onto the dance floor.

"You're dancing again."

"What?" Startled, Danai turned and found Makhosini standing next to her. "I saw you out there busting some nice moves with Nyika." Makhosini's lips twitched in amusement.

"Yes, Makhosini," she laughed. "I'm dancing again."

"If I ask, will you dance with me?" he teased.

"If you ask"—her eyes swept over his tall form—"I might follow you."

Makhosini chuckled at her boldness. "Dance with me, Danai," he whispered. Without waiting for a reply, he clasped her hand and led her toward the dance floor.

Zapp and Roger's melody ripped through the atmosphere: "I wanna be your man."

"I just wanna be your—" Zapp groaned, and Danai placed her arms around Makhosini's neck.

"It's nice seeing you smile again." He inhaled her flowery scent and moved closer. "How have you been, Little Girl?"

"I've been fine." She laughed at the strange irony. She was dancing with the man who had initiated all the turmoil. "Lilly told me about Melissa. Are you okay?"

"Your man, your man, I just wanna be—" Roger's voice saturated the atmosphere, and the crowd crumbled. Makhosini shut his eyes and drew Danai closer in his arms, and the world around them disappeared.

"I don't know why everyone is acting like I suffered some great tragedy," Danai whispered to the closed eyes.

"You? Never," he mused, "but him maybe."

"Wait! What?" Danai's eyes widened, "Makhosini, you knew about Daniel?" Her question ripped through the music. Makhosini shifted uncomfortably but remained silent. Fire kindled deep within Danai. Memories of the events following their kiss flooded her senses.

"You knew about Daniel and kissed me," she muttered in shock. "Why, Makhosini? For fun?"

"Did he ask you what happened?" His words pierced her already wounded heart. "Did he even call you?"

It was true that Daniel hadn't called her, but Makhosini's words fanned the fire rising within her. "You know what, Makhosini, because of your childish game, I messed up the most important thing in my life. You're just like Daniel."

"No, Little Girl, I'm not like your little boy. Because I would never have let you go."

"Whatever, Makhosini," Danai hissed and watched him walk away.

"He's right, you know." Lillian gave Danai an apologetic look. "Daniel should have trusted you enough to at least hear you out."

"What?" Danai blurted. *How long had her aunt been standing there?* Embarrassed, Danai walked off the dance floor to avoid Lillian's gaze.

"Ladies and gents, we'll be closing in ten minutes. You don't have to go home but you gotta get out of here," DJ Tonite hollered over the mic. A boisterous Nyika led the way out of Silk Factory and down the elaborate stairway. As the crew descended, Danai grabbed Makhosini's arm.

"Why did you do it?" she demanded.

"I wanted you," he said.

"What?" Danai choked in disbelief. "That's just crazy, Makhosini."

78

"I know." He ran his fingers over his eyes and broke into a boyish grin.

Danai did not know why she burst into laughter. When she looked up again, Makhosini was laughing, too. In the distance, the crowd stared in confusion.

"I'm sorry, Danai," Makhosini soothed. Sincerity filled his eyes. His boyish grin gave the navy-blue suit a softer appearance. "I never meant to hurt you. Will you forgive me, Little Girl?" Makhosini placed a soft kiss on Danai's open palm.

"I'm dancing again." She inhaled the night's air and ignored curious onlookers.

"What?" Makhosini's eyes flickered in confusion.

"I'm dancing again." Danai giggled. She placed her fingers into his hand and moved closer. Surprised, Makhosini laughed. Holding her hand firmly, he lit the cigarette hanging from the side of his mouth and led their way out of Silk Factory. And that's how Makhosini Moyo and Danai Matamba began.

Chapter Twelve
Restriction—Baba's Decision

Danai grimaced at the scorching midday sun and adjusted her hat. She stepped onto the school courtyard and strolled through the maze of emerald-green hats.

"Danai! Hi, girl." Shupi stepped out of the shadows and grabbed Danai's sleeve. A notorious bully, Shupi was the root of many students' fears. Today, however, as she clung to Danai's sleeve, Shupi's face looked angelic.

"I like your new hairstyle. It's cool, hey." Shupi pointed at the waterfall of braids. Her voice held an unfamiliar friendliness that caused Danai to shift uncomfortably and reluctantly smile back at the girl. "If you ever need anything, let me know. Okay, little sister." Shupi said, grinning ferociously.

Danai's ten-day school break had ended, and she'd returned to boarding school. Shupi's strange greeting marked the beginning of an onslaught of unusual attention from senior students. The girls invited Danai to sit and talk to them. They asked her opinion on trivial matters. Uncertain of the senior girls' intent, she made quick excuses and walked away. The morning's drama cumulated with the arrival of the Dangerous Duo, Marilyn and Thandiwe. Famous for being Harare's most beautiful girls, Marilyn and Thandiwe's only attribute that exceeded their extraordinary beauty was their wicked personalities. The girls mastered the art of backstabbing and were often at the center of any commotion between students. Today, as the girls stood in front of Danai, both girls were smiling innocently.

"So, Danai, any plans for next weekend?" Thandiwe asked.

"Thandi and me want you and your friends. Your *other* friends," Marilyn spoke out. She shot a disapproving look at Layla and Thulani. "We want you to come to my party next weekend."

"The party's at my house on Saturday. Will you come?" Thandiwe asked.

"I can't," Danai mumbled.

"Why not?" Annoyance swept over Thandiwe's face.

"Oh well, why don't you think about it?" Marilyn proposed.

"And bring your *other* friends," Thandiwe emphasized. The two girls giggled mischievously before rushing off to their next class.

"I can't go even if I wanted to," Danai mumbled to herself. In fact, according to Baba, she wouldn't be going anywhere for a long time.

The morning after Nyika's birthday bash, Danai left Lilly's house and went home. She walked into her bedroom and was unpacking

81

when Baba suddenly stormed into the house. Miles rushed to his bedroom and latched the door shut. From her bedroom window, Danai watched Mr. Chris hurrying out of the kitchen door. Still wearing his apron, the man headed to the garden and pretended to assist the gardener.

"Danai, where are you?" Baba roared. Her bedroom door spun open, and Baba filled the doorway. "Are you crazy? Have you lost your mind?"

Flustered, Danai stared at her father. She had never seen Baba this angry. Unable to speak, her tongue clung to the roof of her mouth.

"You asked your mother if you could spend the night with Lillian at her home. But instead of watching TV there, you two were seen at some party dancing the night away, eeh!" As it turned out, Baba didn't simply have his eyes on Zimbabwe's judicial system, but he also had ears on the streets. "And apparently this isn't the first time, is it?" Baba's lips quivered in anger. His eyes momentarily shifted to the doorway. Baba and Danai watched Miles' shadow scurry down the hallway.

"Your grades are falling. You're in the city all the time." Baba slowly moved around the room. "You're not doing well in school because you are *playing*." He grimaced at the life-size poster of Guy. Danai shuddered as her father's disappointment moved from the poster and rested on her.

"I'm paying thousands of dollars so you can attend that luxury resort of a boarding school, and you are entertaining this world with foolishness!" He shook his head.

"I'm sorry, Baba," Danai blurted.

82

"It stops right here, Danai. Today! Nhasi! And you are grounded. No TV, no telephone, nothing! The only places you'll see for the next two months will be this house and your boarding school. If you are not at school, you're here. Do you understand, Danai?"

"Yes, Baba," Danai whimpered, watching her father pacing the room.

"Just try to mess with me." Baba's nostrils flared back and forth. "I'll pull you out of that luxury school and send you to Kumusha to stay with Tete. Do you want to go and live with Tete?"

"No, Baba," Danai gasped. Fear drained through her face at the threat of being sent to the village to live with Baba's sister. In Harare, it was a common practice to send your out-of-control teenager to live with a relative in the rural areas. With no electricity and the nearest telephone and convenience store an hour's walk away, the entire experience had a decidedly calming effect on rebellious personalities. Baba often mocked this system, but today he wasn't mocking it. He seemed, in fact, to be seriously considering implementing it.

"You know better than this, Danai." Baba shook his head and stormed out of the room.

Danai spent the rest of her midterm break confined to the Matamba residence. To ensure he was obeyed, Baba called the house from his office every afternoon. Besides Baba's daily calls, the phone rang at least once a day. Miles would pick up, and Danai would hear her brother chanting, "She can't come to the phone. She's grounded forever and ever." Miles would pause for a few seconds then loudly giggle. "And *ever!*"

Attempting to escape the isolation gnawing within her, Danai began writing her feelings in an old diary. One afternoon, she walked into her room and found Miles lying on her bed, reading her diary and giggling. Rather than being embarrassed at being discovered, Miles decided to taunt his sister.

Danai reached out and grabbed the first thing she could touch—her brother's neck. Mrs. Matamba heard Miles' scream. After untangling the siblings, Mrs. Matamba glared at her daughter and demanded, "Did you birth him?"

"What? I . . ."

"Did you birth him? No, you didn't. I did. And since I gave birth to him, I'm the only one allowed to kill him." Mrs. Matamba readjusted her blouse. "You're getting out of control, Danai. You better stop this craziness. I don't ever want to catch you with your hands on your brother. Do you hear me?"

Everyone within a ten-mile radius heard her.

The following afternoon, Miles ran into Danai's room. "You've got a phone call, princess, and you owe me five dollars."

Danai followed her brother to the lounge.

"Hi, girl, are you okay?" Lillian sounded like someone had died. "I called a couple of times. By the way, you owe Miles five dollars. Are you okay?"

"Yeah, I'm okay," Danai replied, overjoyed at the sound of Lilly's voice. "It's been crazy. No TV, no telephone. I'm really grounded, Lilly, and Baba is angry."

"I know. He came to my job."

"What? When? What did he say?"

"Probably the same thing he said to you. Okay, we're coming to see you," Lilly insisted. Baba's warning echoed through Danai's mind. A vivid vision of living with her aunt in the rural areas swept through her thoughts.

"Who is 'we'? No, don't do that."

"Ten more seconds," Miles screeched. The two heard Mr. Chris' approaching footsteps. Danai frantically hung up.

The following day, her ten-day break ended.

"I can't even if I wanted to," Danai mumbled to herself. She readjusted her hat and stepped out of the scorching sun back onto the school courtyard. In the distance, Marilyn and Thandiwe weaved through the maze of green hats and laughed loudly as they ran to their next class.

Chapter Thirteen
Peace of Heaven

1989 rapidly came to an end. Christmas came and left just as swiftly, but its sweet scents and vivid colors still lingered in every corner of the Matamba residence.

"What do you mean you want to change this?" Mrs. Matamba demanded, "Chantelle, our New Year's Eve party is tomorrow!" With her hand on her hip, Danai's mother rose from her chair and glared at her sister. "We've always used Rooney's for the tents, tables, and chairs. They do a fantastic job, and I don't see why this is a problem today."

Matamba's annual New Year's bash remained the family's biggest event. For Mr. Matamba, it was an opportunity to expand his growing businesses. Each year, Baba invited his closest friends, potential clients, and most influential colleagues. Mrs. Matamba, on the other hand, opened their home to her entire extended family—over a hundred relatives. The event was especially exciting for her four sisters: Auntie Chastity, Auntie Chipo, Auntie Chantelle, and Auntie Chanel. The sisters coordinated and argued about everything from lavish decorations and decadent menus to the elaborate guest list. This year, Auntie Chantelle insisted on hiring her new in-laws rather than Rooney's. That decision became the source of contention between the five sisters.

"Danai, where are you? Come here. One day it'll be you doing this." The ambitious team insisted she join their weekly planning session.

"I have to help Miles with something," Danai lied.

"What! Sit down, girl," Aunt Chipo barked. "What is this we hear about you being grounded?"

"We all know the story," Aunt Chantelle interjected. "Why make the girl repeat it? It's been over two months. Let it go, sisi Chipo. Besides, Lilly should have known better." Her lips curled in disapproval as she mentioned their youngest sister's name. The other sisters hummed in unison.

"We spoiled Lillian—that's the problem." A hint of spite coated Chantelle's words. "I always told Amai that she should have beaten a little sense into that girl."

"Here." Chipo grabbed a wooden cooking spoon and shoved it into Chantelle's hand. "Take this. If you hurry, you can beat rush hour traffic, get to Lilly's house, give her a good thrashing, and then come back here in time to complete our party planning." She rolled her eyes at her own sarcasm.

"Well, Lilly or no Lilly, who will you blame for the way Danai looks?" The ever-fashionable Aunt Chanel added her two cents. "Danai, you may be grounded but that's no excuse to look a mess. When was the last time you combed your hair? And what's with this multi-stained, wrinkled shirt?"

In the background, Mr. Chris grunted in agreement and placed the finishing touches on a gigantic New Year's cake.

"I thought we were going to talk about your party, not my shirt," Danai mumbled.

"Why don't you first go change and at least comb your hair?" her mother urged.

"If I leave this kitchen, I won't be back," the girl defiantly told her mother. "So, it's me and this wrinkled shirt. Anyway, I'll comb my hair tomorrow for the party."

The aunts surrendered and resumed their discussion on Rooney's versus Chantelle's in-laws.

"Hey, fake Princess." Miles barged into the kitchen. "Someone's here to see you."

"Who? Who is here to see her, Miles?" Aunt Chastity demanded. "Miles, you're lying. You're always bothering your sister. Get out of here!" she ordered. His mother nodded and signaled for him to leave.

"Why would I lie?" Miles shuffled his feet and grinned mischievously. Before long, Miles and the aunts were playfully arguing. In the heat of the humorous batter, the kitchen door opened a second time, and Makhosini's tall frame filled the kitchen entrance. Makhosini smiled, and the aunts became speechless.

"Masikati," he greeted the women. His tall figure glided into the kitchen.

"Masikati," the ladies replied in unison. Danai unconsciously ran her fingers over her hair, wishing she had taken Auntie Chanel's advice.

"And you are?" Danai's mother asked, captivated by the sight of the young man.

Unrestrained, Miles shouted, "This is the new boyfriend!"

"What a gorgeous new boyfriend!" Auntie Chantelle chuckled. "No wonder we quickly forgot the last one. Sit next to me, new boyfriend. And go away, Miles." Her sisters briskly shifted their chairs and made room for the beautiful boy.

"Why are you here?" Danai's voice trembled as she grasped his sleeve.

"Your father asked me to meet him here?" Makhosini's eyes nervously searched the room. "I went to his office last month to see him."

"What? Why did you go there?"

"I wanted to apologize for what happened, but he was busy. He told his secretary that I should meet him here today."

"Young man, I've been waiting to meet you." Baba marched into the kitchen. He shook Makhosini's hand. To the aunts' disappointment, Mr. Matamba ordered Makhosini to follow him.

"Run, new boyfriend, run away, save yourself! Don't be brave—run." Miles' squeaky voice trailed behind the two men. Undeterred, Baba and Makhosini disappeared into the long passageway.

"Brave fellow, that Makhosini," Miles somberly declared. "Unfortunately, he's not as wise as the last guy. That one brought his mother for backup!"

Mr. Chris chuckled, and the aunts hummed in agreement.

A slow hour passed while the two men remained behind the closed doors of Baba's study. The aunts cautiously whispered, and Danai imagined the worst. Eventually, Baba appeared from his study with a satisfied expression. A smiling Makhosini followed him back to the kitchen.

"He's probably agreed to go to UNC Chapel Hill," Miles muttered, and the aunts giggled.

"Aren't you going to get ready?" Baba asked his daughter. "Makhosini came to ask me if he could take you out. Nice meeting you, young man." Without another word, Mr. Matamba left the kitchen. Danai laughed in glee before rushing to her room to comb her hair and change her clothes.

They drove past the newly constructed Harare Sports Arena. Danai stared in awe at the league of track teams competing in the distance. Makhosini's car veered north through Eastlea and the lavish Chisipite suburbs until they turned onto Arcturus' serene roads. The peaceful drive was laced with an awkward silence. Danai realized it was the first time she was alone with Makhosini.

"I like your car," she said, breaking the silence.

"I like it, too." Makhosini grinned and revved the 1990 S-class Mercedes. He drove off the main road onto a dirt road and over an aging wooden bridge. A battered sign declared: "My Peace of Heaven."

Towering trees cleared and gave rise to a clear view of a massive two-story yellow farmhouse. Danai saw a lake in the distance and sighed in appreciation. Makhosini parked next to the yellow house, opened the trunk, and grabbed a woven picnic basket.

"Hey, man, you're back. How was your trip?" A lanky boy with freckles and stringy blond hair appeared at the kitchen door. Four white boys dressed in the prestigious red, white, and gray St. Vincent uniform walked out of the kitchen. The boys appeared to be Makhosini's age.

"Are you going in?" The freckled boy grinned. "Everyone's home."

"No, not today. I'll see you guys next weekend."

"Ah okay, bye." The boys disappeared behind the house. Danai heard a noisy truck driving off onto the dirt road.

"Whose place is this?" Danai followed Makhosini through the luscious field toward a lake. Blossoming shrubs and ripening fruit trees drenched the manicured landscape.

"Family. Friends. Well, friends who've become family." Makhosini grinned at her confusion. He took Danai's hand and held it firmly in his. "The guy with the blond hair, that's Mark. It's his family's home."

In the distance the yellow kitchen door swung open. A heavyset, tall woman in her forties emerged from the house and walked toward the couple. She whisked away wisps of gray-blonde hair from her face and turned to an elderly man standing at the doorway.

"It's Makho," the woman shouted in a strong Afrikaans accent, "And he's brought a friend with him."

"Hi, Mr. Volhaagan," Makhosini shouted toward the house. The man standing in the doorway waved, and the woman continued to walk toward the visitors.

"Hey, when did you guys get back? How was Scotland?" The woman hugged Makhosini.

"Scotland was nice." He smiled at the woman. "We got back last Wednesday. Oh, this is Danai. Danai, this is Mrs. Volhaagan."

With a gleaming smile, Mrs. Volhaagan embraced Danai. "Call me Susanna. I'm Makho's mother's best friend. I'm also Makho's other mother." Her voice danced with the wind. "Welcome to A Peace of Heaven."

While Mrs. Volhaagan chattered, Makhosini pulled a blanket from the basket and laid it out along with containers of assorted fruits and sandwiches. Mrs. Volhaagan finished her greetings and returned to the yellow house. Makhosini lifted a liter bottle of cherry plum juice.

"You remembered!" Danai exclaimed at the sight of her favorite beverage.

"We aim to please." He chuckled.

"Why did you go to Scotland?" Danai settled on the blanket next to Makhosini.

"It was our family vacation. Every year we go to a different country for about three weeks. Last year we went to Nairobi and Nassau, Bahamas. This year was for my sister Tafadzwa's wedding. She moved to Scotland two years ago, and last week she got married on Christmas Eve."

"Really, I didn't know you had a sister. How old is she?" Danai suddenly realized how little she knew about the boy sitting next to her.

"Danai, I have seven older sisters!" Makhosini laughed. "I'm the only boy and youngest child." He watched her giggle. "What's so funny?"

"I just thought of my mother's family. There are seven sisters and one boy. Auntie Chastity, she's the oldest, then Christine, that's my mother. Charlene lives in Germany, then Chipo, Chantelle, Chanel—Lilly's first name is actually Chengetai—and Charlie, he's the youngest. He's my age."

"What's with the Cs and Hs?" he asked.

"Exactly!" Danai grinned, and they both burst into laughter.

They ate in silence amid singing birds, watching ancient trees swaying in the dancing wind. Colorful birds showed off their wings and flew from tree to tree.

"It's so beautiful out here." Danai exhaled.

"Yeah, Zimbabwe's full of baby-paradises," Makhosini commented. "Maybe one day, if you're free, we could discover other places together."

"I'd like that." A gentle breeze rushed through her fingers then fluttered from budding tree to tree. "Makhosini?"

"Yes, Danai."

"How come you didn't call me?" Her eyes avoided his gaze. "I mean, why did you wait so long to come see me? You didn't even call."

"I did call." He shook his head. "I called every day for weeks. Each time Miles answered the phone and told me you couldn't talk to anyone. Later, Lillian explained what happened and that you were grounded for two months. So, I figured I'd just wait and respect your father's decision. You know, try to start out on the right foot with you and your family."

"I didn't know," Danai smiled shyly. "I thought you'd changed your mind about us."

"Never." He wrapped his arms around her and smiled sheepishly. "But I think I got you in a lot of trouble, Little Girl."

"What?" Danai burst into laughter. "No, Makhosini, I got myself in a lot of trouble. I'm the one who chose to spend the night at Lilly's house."

"What were you and Baba talking about earlier?" Danai remembered Baba's sudden decision to release her from his prison.

"Guy stuff."

"Like what guy stuff?" She glanced at the lake's rippling waters.

"Like respecting his daughter and his home. He asked me who I was and about my people, my family. He wanted to know my intentions toward you."

"Really." Danai peered at a blue butterfly playing between red flame lilies. She didn't like Baba knowing more about her boyfriend than she did. "And what are your intentions toward me?"

"Me?" Makhosini winked. "I'm just trying to get to know you, Little Girl. Can I try?"

"Well, that depends." Danai's musical laughter filled the atmosphere. "Can you still dance?" She stood up and extended her hand to him. Makhosini grinned. His gaze followed her sensual lips and the arch of her delicate neck.

"Mmm, I don't know. Let's see." He placed his hand in hers and rose from the blanket. In the enchantment of A Peace of Heaven, Makhosini and Danai danced to the wind's whistling ballad.

The sun glided until it rested behind distant hills. Its fiery orange tones caressed the lake's waters, ignoring the couple strolling hand in hand in its path.

"I missed you a lot, Little Girl." Makhosini walked toward the lake and sat on a carpet of grass at the water's edge.

"I missed you, too, Makho." Danai sat next to him. Together they watched the sky transform herself into shades of red, orange, and purple before the sun set on A Peace of Heaven.

Chapter Fourteen
You Must Be the One

Ain't nothing sweeter than new love.
Sweet smelling,
Succulent.
Dancing with the wind while flowing
through time.
New love is carefree and irresistibly
careless.
Yet, it heals the broken hearted,
Taming young men while old men
become strong again.
Resurrecting dying dreams and making
the impossible possible.
Surely there's nothing sweeter than new
love.
—"Powers of Petals"

"**H**appy New Year." Makhosini scooped Danai into his arms. "Happy 1990, baby."

"Hi Makho." She instinctively pulled down the hem of her skirt. She'd debated between three outfits and eventually settled on a short pink denim skirt that fell into pretty layers of ruffled lace. With its matching cropped jacket, the outfit had seemed like the perfect choice. Now Danai wondered if the skirt was too short and the jacket too tight. Maybe she shouldn't have worn the bright red lipstick.

"You look beautiful." Makhosini's soft voice erased her unspoken anxiety as his eyes appreciatively swept over her body.

"I like this," Makhosini confided as they entered Avondale's Majestic Movie Theater. "No shouting people, no crying babies. Today this theater is ours!" He grinned and waved a greeting to an elderly couple seated in the far-right corner. *Neria*, the newly released Zimbabwean film, began. Danai surveyed Makhosini's silhouette. Although his eyes remained focused on the screen, she had the distinct feeling that his mind was elsewhere. He held the look of a man contemplating a life-changing choice, but he didn't utter a word until the movie ended.

"Can you believe it's 1990, Makho?"

"I know, right? It feels almost unreal." Makhosini thoughtfully ran his fingers through his hair and paced his footsteps behind Danai's. "Man, it feels just like yesterday when Nyika, Derek, and I were eleven-year-old boys racing BMX bikes in the mud."

"You raced bikes in the mud?"

"Yes, we did. And I got all these scars to prove it."

She laughed as he lifted his arm and proudly showed off a tiny scar. He opened the door to Gigi's Italian Bakery Café.

"How was your mother's New Year's Eve bash?" Makhosini smiled at Danai's expression as she looked around the restaurant.

"Oh, it was amazing! The aunts really outdid themselves this year." She settled into a chair. "Almost three hundred guests and everything was on point. The music, the catering, even the parking!"

"So, what did you do the entire night? Did you assist the dynamic planning committee?" Makhosini teased.

"Of course I did." Danai giggled at his description of her mother and aunts. Her eyes slowly surveyed the café. The place was tiny, but the rustic gold and aqua couches, large cushions, and glowing candles gave the restaurant an appealing ambiance.

"Wow, I like this place! Do you come here a lot?"

"I do." Makhosini chuckled and pointed to a secluded corner. "I like to sit over there and listen to music or read a book."

"Really?" Danai's gaze shifted to the large glass fridge caging an enormous black currant cake surrounded by fresh cream cannoli, tiramisu squares, and other delightful delicacies. "And how was the party you guys went to?"

"Same old!" Makhosini shook his head, smiling. "Nyika insisted that we stop at his uncle's home before going to Nyangee's party. His uncle has this small family gathering every year. We sat through three hours of unrehearsed speeches by Nyika's relatives. By the time we finally escaped and made it to Nyangee's and Roger's joint, it was two a.m.! The party had already ended, and everyone was leaving. So, we

98

drove back home." He covered his eyes with his hand, and Danai burst into laughter.

A hostess appeared carrying a sample tray of appetizers.

"Are you ready for life after Richlorne High?" Danai asked Makhosini, smiling at the hostess.

"I'm trying to be." Makhosini's eyes soaked in her presence. "It's hard to believe this is going to be my final year of high school, but it's been great while it lasted. Are you ready for your O-level year?"

"I don't know." She grimaced as she remembered her latest report card. "I have a lot of catching up to do. Do you know what you're going to do after high school?" Danai realized that she sounded like her father, but Makhosini didn't seem to notice.

"Probably go to university. I want to become a business strategist." He grinned.

"A what?"

"Oh, business strategist is a concept that me and my mentor came up with," he explained, tasting his mango strawberry cheesecake. "It's like being a business surgeon or a company creator. I want to work with businesses to figure out things like where's the best place to open their company. Will their product flourish in that specific area?"

"You mean sort of like a company planner?"

"Yeah, that's it. It'd be cool to help businesses start out and collaborate with companies that are failing. I like the challenge of understanding what went wrong and fixing it." His finger brushed hers as he reached for a bite-size chocolate cannoli. "What about you, Little Girl? What's your passion? What you gon' be?"

"Well—" Her eyes shifted in hesitation. Danai had never confided her dream to anyone. "Art is my passion. I can draw nonstop for hours. When I'm creating, I feel so alive."

"Really! What type of art do you create?"

Makhosini's interest surprised her. "I'm a born painter. My favorite media is oil paints. I like the texture and vibrancy of oil paints. I'm convinced that there's no experience or feeling that can't be captured by oil paint." She giggled at Makhosini's doubtful expression. "To be honest, I'm still trying to discover myself as an artist. Last year, I took a pottery class, and I've been doing African batiks for almost two years now."

"Wow, that's really cool!" Makhosini looked impressed.

"It's what I want to do. My dream. My passion!" she confessed. "But Baba believes the only rich artist is a dead artist. He wants me to go to University of Zimbabwe or UNC Chapel Hill and become a lawyer like him or a doctor like his cousin, Uncle Farai."

"And what do you want?" He carefully watched as she drew a design on a paper napkin.

"I guess I want to create art and make money from it. I know it's possible."

"So, my girlfriend's going to be a famous artist, mmm." Makhosini grinned sheepishly. "And when do I get to see some of these masterpieces?"

Danai smiled. She liked the way he'd called her his girlfriend. The waiter appeared carrying a second tray of assorted desserts. In the quiet intimacy of Gigi's Italian Bakery, Makhosini and Danai shared mango cheesecake while listening to the sultry sounds of Sade.

100

"Everything's changing." Danai stared at the increasing traffic as they drove through the city. Bright city lights and freshly painted billboards revamped aging buildings. Harare had awakened and was growing.

Everything has changed, and nothing will ever be the same again, she thought. She'd never imagined Daniel and she would end, but they had. Her eyes flickered toward Makhosini. *I'm really starting to like this guy, but I'm scared that one day we'll change, too.* She glanced out of the window and watched desperate pedestrians weaving through relentless traffic. Makhosini switched on the radio, and Danai's heart leaped at the sound of Regina Belle crooning, "It Doesn't Hurt Anymore."

On January 1st, 1990, Danai Matamba became new again.

Thunder raged and lightning swept through a pitch-black sky. Danai stood at the doorway and waved as Makhosini drove out of the courtyard. The night's wind howled, forcing the Matambas' main door to abruptly shut.

"Danai, is that you?" A voice pierced the confusion. Aunt Chastity stared through the window at a hundred-year-old tree swaying in the distance. "Danai?" her voice echoed behind her niece's footsteps.

Startled, Danai entered the house and swerved. Her mud-caked shoe slipped off her foot. "Maneru. Good evening," she muttered and entered the living room. Her eyes flickered from her parents to Aunt Chastity, who sat next to a coffee table at the far end of the room. Mr. Matamba's gaze momentarily rested on his daughter before he resumed watching the eight o'clock evening news.

"Danai, when was the last time you spoke to Monique?" Aunt Chastity observed her niece.

"More than a year ago, I think," Danai mumbled into an unsettling silence.

"Did she ever mention a boy called Dumelo?" her aunt's interrogation began.

"No."

"You're sure she didn't say anything to you?"

"No, Auntie."

"Nothing? Did you know your cousin is pregnant? At fifteen, pregnant!" The woman groaned with her announcement. The windy rain defiantly pushed open the main door while a windowpane violently rattled. "She's only a year younger than you, and you're telling me that she didn't say anything to you?"

"No, Maiguru." Danai staggered at her aunt's words. At the tender age of seven, Monique had appeared at the Matambas' doorstep. Danai remembered the night she awoke to someone pounding on the main door. Her mother opened the door and gasped in shock at the scantily dressed girl standing next to a large mustard suitcase. Danai had remained hidden in a dark corner of the living room. Stupefied, she'd watched Aunt Chastity hurriedly rush off and board a raggedy minivan. Without a second glance, Aunt Chastity and her third husband drove off into the night, leaving Monique standing at the doorway.

Monique grew up a quiet, thoughtful girl, considerate of others but apprehensive about life. "When I grow up, I'm going to be Zimbabwe's first woman pilot. Then I'll never be poor again, and I can fly away to a faraway place," she'd wistfully confided in Danai. Fascinated by the younger girl's ingenuity, Danai pledged to go with her. Monique seemed to know things that Danai had grown up

102

shielded from. The two girls became inseparable, sharing clothes and secrets.

Aunt Chastity had returned alone four years later. Impoverished and heartbroken, she had picked up Monique and returned to the life and home she'd once deserted. No one spoke of those tumultuous years and the events that led to Aunt Chastity abandoning her only child. Danai had not seen Monique in three years, but a vision of the scantily dressed girl, now fifteen and carrying a baby, overpowered Danai's senses. Dismayed, she wept.

"Aah, what will you do, sisi?" Mrs. Matamba's sympathy rested on her oldest sister.

"The school's already expelled Monique." Aunt Chastity's eyes reluctantly moved from her sister to her brother-in-law until her downcast gaze fell toward the floor. "They sent her home. She's at home right now as we speak."

"And the boy? Have you spoken to his family?"

"Sisi, we have spoken to the family. But what can be done? Bride price will be paid. Monique and Dumelo will have a traditional wedding next month before this baby's born." Like a sword, Aunt Chastity's eyes mercilessly shifted, piercing the girl who stood awkwardly in the center of the room. "I don't know how you girls can be so foolish. You're dancing with fire and praying you won't get burnt. You're playing around with these little boys and throwing away the rest of your lives. Look at your cousin. Monique is a child, and now she's having a child and marrying a child." Tears raged down Aunt Chastity's cheeks. "Dumelo is only sixteen!"

Outside the wind abruptly eased, and the rain's gentle melody invaded the silence. Aunt Chastity stared into the night's unrelenting darkness through a half-closed window. Despair flooded her face while dark shadows and wrinkles burrowed into her once-perfect skin. Danai's aunt appeared to have aged overnight.

"My daughter's become a mother even before she's become a woman," Aunt Chastity wailed in agony. The sound of her anguish filled and suffocated the entire house. "Is this what you girls call love, Danai?"

Thunder roared. Rushing wind pounded on a windowpane, and the battle outside resumed.

Love? A single tear rolled down Danai's cheek. Images of Daniel rushed through her mind. Baba looked up at his daughter and shifted uncomfortably. He, too, was remembering the awkward boy who'd appeared at their home six months ago. The boy professed his unrelenting love while hiding behind an overbearing mother. Baba watched sadness invade his only daughter's eyes. For a second, the two became unified in the memory of Danai's unspoken agony and forgot that Monique was pregnant.

"Answer me, Danai!" Aunt Chastity's screech tore through the room. "Is this what you girls call love?"

Chapter Fifteen
"School Time"

❦

"What?" Danai choked on a piece of bacon. "What did you say, Baba?"

It had been a month since Aunt Chastity's shocking revelation. Monique had married Dumelo in a quick union under the shadows of many relatives hastily exchanging gifts. In the aftermath of these events, a strange calm settled over the Matamba residence. Danai skillfully avoided her parents, but Baba's announcement at breakfast disrupted the fragile truce.

"Mrs. Patel or Makhosini. That's the deal. You choose!" Faithful to his morning routine, Baba folded the *Financial Gazette* and dug into a plate of eggs and toast.

"But Baba, Makhosini says you asked him to be my tutor?" She bit into a piece of toast and swallowed her humiliation.

"Yes, I did." Baba's attention moved from the plate to his daughter.

"But why? Makhosini is my friend. Why would you tell him about my grades?" Embarrassment rippled down Danai's cheeks.

"Because Danai, you haven't been doing well in school for over a year. Your grades are falling, and you're failing." Mr. Matamba watched his daughter's dejected expression. "O-level season is almost here. Those exams are the most important exams of your life. Without them, you'll be kicked out of high school and end up a high school dropout."

Father and daughter sat on opposite sides of the dining table, glaring at each other. In silence, they considered the boy who'd glided into their lives and now challenged their relationship.

"By the way, I have never discussed your grades with Makhosini or anyone else. I simply asked him if he would be interested in tutoring you." Mr. Matamba smothered his toast in marmalade. "He did very well at his O-levels, you know. Nine As and two Bs!" Pride coated Baba's voice.

"But why him?"

"Economics, my dear!" Baba took a sip of bitter grapefruit juice. "What is the first premise of economics?"

"The first premise of economics?" Danai repeated, momentarily disorientated. "It's supply and demand. If there is no demand, we create the demand so we can supply a need," she quoted *World Economics*, a book Baba had forced all members of the Matamba household to read.

"Exactly! You see whether you admit it or not, you have a demand. Your demand is you want to see this Makhosini. I have a demand that

I want you to pass your O-level exams with flying colors and go on to university. Makhosini is our supply." He chuckled.

"And what if I refuse?" Danai carefully watched her father.

"If you refuse?" Baba's teeth ripped into a piece of toast. "Then it's Mrs. Patel, every Saturday morning for the rest of the year."

Danai frowned as an image of Mrs. Patel floated into her thoughts. She grimaced at the memory of her first encounter with the woman.

Two years earlier, Mr. Matamba had received Danai's semiannual report card in the mail. Next to each subject was the word "excellent." Her mathematics teacher had simply penned "exceptional." On his next visit to the school, Baba had desperately searched for the math teacher and asked her to define "exceptional."

"Well, Mr. Matamba, your daughter has a rare and very real gift," the teacher had confided. "And, if she continues to grow in it, she could be moved to advanced math classes, which as you know, will not only facilitate her entry to a good university but help her SAT preparation."

Riding on the delight of this gift, Mr. Matamba had immediately secured the services of a private tutor—Mrs. Patel.

Born in Masvingo, a southeastern province of Zimbabwe, Amina Rae Patel deserted her hometown on her eighteenth birthday. Two days later, she entered the prestigious University of Zimbabwe where she received a Bachelor of Mathematics. On her graduation day, Amina put away the degree and married the honorable Dr. S. D. Patel. They had a seven-day wedding ceremony for a marriage that would last over five decades. Mrs. Patel adopted a new name and the title of mother and wife. Twenty-four years later, that role became obscure

107

when the last of her children left her home to pursue their own careers.

Lost in transition, Mrs. Patel returned to her lost passion. She rearranged her life and her home to offer services as a math tutor. Mrs. Patel's excellence became renowned and her services highly sought after. Once a week, on Saturday mornings, she opened two large rooms of her home to accommodate the hopelessly incompetent and the exceptionally gifted. Unfortunately, Mrs. Patel didn't simply teach mathematics, she majored in boredom. For two gruesome hours, Mrs. Patel spoke in a soft monotone voice, thereby transforming the fascinating world of mathematics into unforgettable torture.

"The early bird always catches the worm," Mrs. Patel insisted. Her Saturday morning lessons began promptly at 7:30 a.m. She conducted her lessons in the main dining room where she could easily split her attention between Danai and Dr. Patel eating his breakfast. The monotony of her morning lessons was only interrupted by the gentle swish of her colorful sari. Every Saturday, Mrs. Patel wore a different sari. Woven in fine fabric and rich delicate threads, each sari revealed the story of its weaver. The rich colors gave Mrs. Patel's face a fresh and youthful glow and Danai marveled at the perfection of the intricate embroidery.

"From South Africa, you know, Danai," she excitedly confided about the origin of each sari.

At 7:55 a.m., Dr. S. D. Patel would send Mrs. Patel to the master bedroom for a different handkerchief or tie. Upon her departure, the man would frantically rise from the table and sneak a samosa or other sweet delicacies into Danai's hands.

"You must survive. Good luck to you," he sympathetically declared as he hastily made his escape. Dr. Patel swiftly defected through the side door, sprung into his 1979 Mercedes, and drove off to freedom. Mrs. Patel would return holding the tie or another handkerchief. Unperturbed, she would gently shut the side door and continue her monotone lessons.

"Failure is never an option." Faithful to her motto, Mrs. Patel refused to become enticed into any other topic of conversation than math. Failure hadn't been an option for her four daughters who'd graduated as surgeons from the University of Cape Town, and according to Mrs. Patel, failure could never be an option for Danai, her student. Unfortunately, boredom was.

Baba watched Danai silently weighing her options: Mrs. Patel versus Makhosini.

"So, Makhosini it is! Lessons begin next week. Every Saturday morning at my office," Baba triumphantly exclaimed. He laid down his butter knife and rose from the table. "And Danai, as long as I'm your father, you're not going to end up like your cousin Monique."

To Mr. Matamba's delight and his daughter's disappointment, Danai's tutoring lessons progressed well. Makhosini arrived early every Saturday morning and met father and daughter at Matamba and Associates law office. For two hours, the ever-calm Makhosini taught patiently and answered Danai's multitude of questions. Eventually, Danai found herself looking forward to their Saturday sessions.

"I'm impressed, Danai," Makhosini grinned, holding up her latest pretest. "We're a force to be reckoned with."

"What?" She grabbed the paper and stared at her grade. "Yes, I guess we are truly a force to be reckoned with."

Chapter Sixteen
Funny Love

Where does Love run to?

In the confines of midnight's hour,

Where does my love rest his head?

Does he flow soft as Zambezi's waves?

Or roar like Victoria's Waterfalls?

Parading himself like summer lightning,

Will Love consume me?

—"Powers of Petals"

"August eighteenth, 1990, St. Vincent rugby team versus the Richlorne Springbucks." That announcement blasted through every radio station and soaked the airwaves. Despite the day's monstrous heat, Harare Sports Arena roared with enthusiastic supporters of all ages. Over twelve thousand fans and curious bystanders had turned up for the final game of Harare's regional high school rugby. This year the annual tournament, which had initially begun as a friendly competition between various high school rugby teams, had become the year's largest social event. An unprecedented gathering of people from all walks of life.

In the weeks preceding the game, Richlorne and St. Vincent High engaged in outrageous off-the-field battles. Rumors of girlfriend stealing, verbal confrontations, and the disappearance of St. Vincent's mascot spread like wildfire. As the pregame battle raged, police were called in. The perpetrators were sons of respected business owners, doctors, and prominent politicians. Harare's news media caught wind of the boys' unscrupulous exploits, and within days the annual game transformed from a simple rugby match to the center of national media coverage. Spectators and ardent fans filled the stadium to witness a war destined to end all battles.

"These boys better represent. They better win," Nyika shouted. He adjusted his waistcoat and followed Godfrey, Derek, and Makhosini onto the bleachers. "Man, if they lose, I'm through with Richlorne High."

St. Vincent's team and the Richlorne Springbucks stood on opposite ends of the field, scrutinizing each other. Suddenly there was a resounding sound. The huddle pushed, and war began. St Vincent's Edwin Banda appeared out of nowhere and tackled Richlorne's rising star, Ticha Shungu. With a loud thump, both boys landed on the ground. From the stands, Makhosini looked up to see Danai and Lillian ascending the bleachers next to theirs. Danai frowned and looked away. Annoyed that her boyfriend had disappeared after their tutoring session and opted to go to the game with the boys rather than her, Danai avoided his gaze.

"What's wrong? What happened?" Lilly's eye flickered from Danai to Makhosini in the distance.

"Lately Makhosini says he wants to hang out with the boys. He quickly packs up and leaves as soon as we finish studying." Danai pouted and followed Lilly onto a vacant row. "At first I didn't mind, but now it's happening all the time." Both girls looked up and watched Makhosini in the distance.

"Did you talk to him about it?" Lilly asked.

"I've tried. He says I wouldn't understand and that it's a guy thing. Today we got into an argument. I told him if things don't change, I'm breaking up with him. Then he can be single and really date his boys." She sat next to Lilly.

"What?" Lilly laughed and shook her head, "Well, if Makhosini is too busy to hang out with you, maybe you should get too busy to hang out with him. It works all the time." They both stared at Godfrey, grinning in the distance.

Ticha leaped to his feet, retrieved the ball, and ran. The boy breezed like the wind, leaping over the human wall rushing toward him. He stumbled, then quickly regained his balance and raced ahead of the mob of players pursuing him.

"Eeh, this boy is running like a man in love," a man yelled from the bleachers. Makhosini turned his attention to his girl—captured in the wave of excitement, Danai jumped up and cheered.

With the ball firmly in his bosom, Ticha spun to avoid his attackers. The audience exploded into frenzied applause. With lightning speed, Ticha sprinted toward the goal posts and gracefully laid the ball between the two posts. Astounded, the boisterous crowd rose to their feet and roared.

Makhosini pushed his way through the cheering crowd, and Danai turned and found him standing next to her. Without a word, Makhosini wrapped his arms around Danai and held her close. Surprised, she giggled and held him tightly. Within a blink, her uninhibited joy transformed into unspoken fear, and Danai began crying. Tears shamelessly streamed down her face. *I think I've fallen in love with this man,* she thought. *When he smiles, I will laugh, and if he cries, I'll fall apart.*

"Hey sisi, stop this drama." A man standing next to the couple roughly nudged Danai's shoulder. "It's just a rugby game! Stop this crying."

Ignoring the irate man, Danai held Makhosini tighter—*If he cries, I'll fall apart.*

True to their legacy, St. Vincent won the game and retained their victory trophy. Ticha Shungu walked off the field carrying the prestigious Player of the Year award. Despite Richlorne High's loss, the Springbucks gained new fame and the audience's respect.

"Man, I'm so through with Richlorne." Nyika spat. "After we graduate this year, they better never call me asking for alumni donations and whatnot."

114

Chapter Seventeen
Zimbabwean Storm

Like a turbulent storm, O-level exam season descended on sub-Saharan Africa. Parents throughout the Sunshine City panicked, joining millions of parents around the world. Mr. Matamba wasn't taking any chances. He promptly announced a barrage of new house rules. The tedious list included limiting Danai's phone calls to fifteen minutes per day and an hour of television on weekends. The aunts quietly relocated their weekly New Year's Bash meeting to Aunt Chanel's home in Eastlea. To escape Baba's onslaught of restrictive regulations, Miles disappeared on Saturdays, opting to spend his weekends with Uncle Farai and his family.

At school, stress levels escalated to new heights. With less than two months before the first exam, students aggressively searched for any place with enough privacy to study. Girls gathered under trees, squeezed into study rooms, and hid in bathrooms. As tensions mounted, study aids mysteriously disappeared and more arguments broke out between students. Simple misunderstandings rapidly progressed to heated quarrels. Close friends became new foes, while old enemies united in an effort to tackle the dreaded exams. One afternoon, Layla walked into the cafeteria and found her chemistry partner in a secluded corner. The girl lay sprawled on the floor clutching a pile of books.

"I can't do this anymore, Layla. I just can't!" She wept into the floor tiles.

Mr. Ritchie, the school's headmaster did little to ease the mounting anxiety. "No pressure, ladies," he assured the students during their final assembly. "Simply remember two things as you prepare. Firstly, it is an honor to sit for and take the O-level exam. Secondly, failure is always public information. Basically, we'll all know!" He closed his book and walked off the podium.

"Hey, girls." Sibo's braided head appeared at Thulani's bedroom door. Surprised, Layla looked up and closed her physics study manual. Her eyes darted to Danai, sitting at Thulani's desk. Both girls glanced at Thulani, who lay on her bed eating ice cream and flipping through *Drum* magazine's fashion must-haves.

"What happened? Aren't you guys speaking to me?" Sibo laughed cheerily.

"I think we're surprised to see you." Layla watched Sibo. "We hardly see you anymore."

"I've been busy preparing for these wretched O-levels, and when I'm free, I hang out with Sharice and her crew." Sibo chuckled. Her friends looked troubled, but Sibo strutted further into the room and flopped on the bed next to Thulani. "Sharice asked me to invite you guys to her room tonight so we can all catch up on the latest news."

Known as the Tattlers, Sharice and her crew earned the name by delving into other people's lives. With a swiftness that exceeded local intelligence agencies, the Tattlers gathered information on students and their families. Their tactics were seamless and left no stone unturned. Other students' secrets became common knowledge in the mouths of these fearless girls. The Tattlers' greatest feat had been the Miss Lye incident earlier this year. In the hope of ousting Mr. Ritchie, the school's deputy headmistress, Miss Lye, secretly colluded with the Tattlers. The devious deputy lured the crew with expensive dinners and promises of securing future scholarships to overseas universities. Through these strategic methods, Miss Lye urged the wayward girls to gather damaging information on Mr. Ritchie. A month into the strange collaboration, the school's disciplinary committee charged Miss Lye with insubordination and promptly fired her. A decision based solely on reports made by Sharice and the Tattlers. That evening, Danai, Thulani, Layla, and a handful of other students gathered in Sharice's room. Perplexed, the girls listened as Sharice and her friends boasted about their true intent. As it turned out, the crew's goal from the onset of the ghastly affair had been to rid their school of the unpopular deputy headmistress!

With the arrival of O-level season, Sharice and her crew routinely exposed Honor students' study routines. As a result, the Tattlers' popularity soared to new heights.

"So, are you guys coming?" Sibo asked.

Danai and Layla exchanged wary glances.

"You guys go. I'm not coming." Thulani sat up.

"Why, what's up?" Sibo asked.

"I don't want to go to Sharice's room. I'm tired of talking about other people's misery. It's gossip, Sibo." Thulani's soft musical voice reprimanded her friend.

"I agree," Layla blurted. "Besides, when we leave, they'll probably talk about us, too."

"Well, I think Sharice and them are cool," Sibo insisted. "Besides, we used to go to their room, and I don't see why this year should be any different."

"Exactly, Sibo, we once did it—but why?" Thulani asked. She glanced at her friends' blank expressions, now fully focused on her. "I mean, guys, are our own lives so empty that we need to chew up other people's lives to feel good about ourselves?"

"Okay, Miss High and Mighty," Sibo hissed and rose from the bed. "It was okay when you used to do it. Now it's suddenly a sin. Ever since you started dating that Giles, you think you're better than all of us, eeh!"

The two girls launched into a heated argument. Layla and Danai watched in bewilderment as their friends argued about everything from Thulani's new boyfriend to Sibo's past actions.

"You can believe whatever you want to, Sibo, but like I said, I'm not coming," Thulani shouted in frustration.

"She says she's not coming," Layla echoed.

"Whatever, shut up, Layla!" Sibo retorted and walked toward the door. "Danai, are you coming?"

"Nope." Danai chuckled. "All that crap I went through last year and my changing hairstyles this year should keep Sharice and her friends busy for the whole night."

Enraged, Sibo stormed out of the room and headed for Sharice's room.

"I think we just lost a friend." Layla chuckled and shook her head.

Danai looked at her friends. Something she couldn't explain had changed. "I think we're finally growing up," she mumbled, reopening her math study aid.

"It looks like it's just the three of us from now on." Thulani swallowed a spoonful of coconut ice cream and turned back to *Drum*'s fashion must-haves.

Ten exams were randomly spread over an eight-week period. With less than six weeks before the first exam, Layla, Thulani, and Danai increased their study schedule. They read Macbeth before dawn and studied African history during lunch. The girls trailed through World Geography after their afternoon classes. While the rest of the world slept, Layla, Thulani, and Danai oscillated between physics and math.

On a rainy November afternoon, Danai walked into the school's art pavilion. Sixteen students sat on randomly placed stools throughout the room. Danai chose a seat next to an open window. The examiner introduced himself before unveiling their exam assignment. In the center of the pavilion sat a voluptuous woman draped in an elaborate head wrap and a flowing traditional African dress. A bell rang, and O-Levels began. The students' brush strokes danced over their canvases until the woman seated in front of them became the image on their canvases. African jazz filled the room, matching the boisterous movements of many paintbrushes. With each stroke of her brush, Danai's anxiety evaporated. Four hours later, she rose from her stool.

"One exam down." Danai exhaled, "Nine more to go!" She grabbed her paintbrushes and walked out of the art pavilion.

Chapter Eighteen
Heaven's Diamonds

T hey came like diamonds falling from heaven. One drop, then another, until drops of water became rain showers on thirsty land. The storm soaked everything in sight and ended the drought of 1990. Gushing water rummaged through gutters, washing Harare's streets and alleys. The angry rain aggressively swept away the final traces of 1990, and a new year began.

"O-level results are out!" Shouts echoed from Mbare's flea markets to the Business District.

"Zvanzi mazamini abuda!" Cries from the villages broke into the stillness of sleeping suburbs. Anxious parents and hopeful students gathered outside the headmaster's suite. Mr. Matamba marched into Mr. Ritchie's office. Without a word, he briskly signed his name, grabbed an envelope, and marched out with his daughter in tow.

Before they made it to his car, Mr. Matamba frantically tore open the large envelope. Motionless, he stood and stared at a piece of paper. His eyes slowly flickered from one row to the next. Shocked, he covered his mouth with his hand and began weeping. Dismayed, Danai stared at her father. She had never seen Baba cry, so she began crying, too.

"Danai, you passed," her father uttered between his sobs. "You passed! All your subjects, you passed and did so well."

Stunned, Danai grabbed the paper from Baba and slowly read each row. With tears rolling down his face, Mr. Matamba watched his daughter dancing amidst the diamond raindrops.

"I passed!" Layla screamed. "Danai, can you believe I passed?" She raced toward the car, hurled her results at Mr. Matamba, and grabbed Danai's report.

"We both made it!" the delighted Layla exclaimed. "And guess what, Thulani made Honors. Our girl got ten As!" The two girls hugged each other and leaped in the rain.

"Congratulations, Layla! You girls did very well." Mr. Matamba shook Layla's hand. "Come on, Danai, let's go home. We must tell Mbuya and your mother. Also, we need to call Uncle Farai and your aunties."

"Baba, there's somewhere I need to go. Can I come home later?" Danai pleaded.

Mr. Matamba looked at the results in his hand and nodded.

"I can't believe your parents agreed to this." Danai unbuckled her seat belt and leaned into the backseat of Thulani's Mini Cooper.

"They didn't." Thulani smiled into the rearview mirror. "I told them I was spending the night at your house."

"What?" Danai's gaze shot up to meet her friends.

"Me too!" Layla opened the passenger door and stepped out of the car. "I even packed two pairs of pajamas as proof for my stepmother. Wait! Who's paying for this excursion?"

"Stop worrying, Layla." Thulani laughed at her friend's alarmed expression. "We came here to celebrate us passing O-levels. Besides, Godfrey and Lilly are paying for this."

The girls turned and watched Godfrey's yellow Mazda ascending the winding driveway.

"Are you kidding me? You guys got me out here treading through wildlife?" Nyika scooted out of the Mazda's backseat. He bent over to adjust his khaki shorts. "This is exactly what I'm talking about!" Nyika frantically pointed at a heap of knee-high elephant dung. Recovering his composure, he stood upright and stared at a gigantic baobab tree. The tree's broad trunk and root-like branches appeared to extend for miles. A subtle squeal escaped Nyika lips. Dismayed, his eyes strained at a pride of lions basking under the baobab tree.

"Good afternoon, I'm Beatrice." A park ranger walked toward the group, laughing at Nyika's theatrics. "Welcome to Pamuzinda Safari Lodge."

Beatrice climbed into an open-sided Land Cruiser and beckoned the visitors to jump in.

"So, where did you tell your father you were going?" Layla settled on a seat next to Danai and Makhosini.

"I told him I was spending the afternoon at your house." Danai grinned mischievously. "No one is crazy enough to call your house."

"Just a few reminders before we begin our journey." Beatrice's eyes swept over the group. "Remember to stay in your seats while the vehicle's moving. The animals we'll encounter consider this van as part of their normal habitat. If you suddenly stand up, it could be perceived as a challenge." She glanced at a lioness approaching the vehicle. "And please refrain from attempting to stroke or feed the lions." The girls turned to stare at Nyika, who clung to his seat in the rear. The lioness continued to pace behind the Land Cruiser.

"It feels like we've entered another world," Danai exclaimed. The vehicle veered forward onto a rocky terrain.

"Yep, I still can't believe this place is only two hours from the city." Makhosini moved closer to her.

"Guys, look at that!" Lilly pointed at a journey of giraffes in the distance.

"Giraffes are our most popular species," Beatrice bellowed over the Cruiser's microphone. "Can you believe that they only sleep for thirty minutes a day? Giraffes can go three weeks without drinking water!" The group stared in awe at the long-necked herbivores.

The van plunged deeper into the savannah landscape. Flat-topped acacia trees and fruit-filled shrubbery interrupted the virgin landscape. As the Cruiser charged forward, a herd of long-mane zebras rushed past the moving vehicle.

"Look, that one has no stripes. It's a white zebra!" Danai exclaimed. The ground shook violently, and the visitors gasped as an assemblage of antelope followed suit.

"Impala, Sable, Kudu!" Thulani jumped to her feet. "That's Eland!" She quickly sat back down, and Beatrice slowed the Cruiser.

"How do you know?" Godfrey watched the population of African antelope.

"The unique coloring, and look at the different horns," Thulani explained.

"Give it up for our ten-A princess," Layla shouted, and the group erupted into a torrent of cheers.

With inexplicable agility, a cheetah slid down the trunk of an acacia tree. Its slender form bolted through the torrent of antelope. Unrestrained, the cheetah sped toward its target in the distance. Sensing danger, a congregation of hyenas regrouped and prepared for the approaching confrontation. The cheetah lunged forward within the circle of hyenas, and a battle reminiscent of a territorial dance broke out. With surprising swiftness, the cheetah thrust toward the dominant male, challenging the congregation's hierarchy. The mob of hyenas moved in slow purposeful movements then erupted into haunting laughter. The pack's leader grasped its opponent between its robust jaws. Startled, the cheetah writhed violently until it catapulted itself into the air and landed back on its feet.

"Aah!" The visitors collectively gasped and rose from their seats. A short distance from the fight, trees quivered and branches rustled as a second tremor shook the earth. Through the thick greenery, a parade of elephants appeared. The hyenas stiffened in fear and immediately dispersed, bringing the dispute to an end. Relieved, the cheetah scurried back to its cubs that were playing under the acacia tree.

"I thought she was instigating a fight, but I guess she was trying to protect her family." Derek chuckled, and his friends hummed in agreement.

The elephants moved steadily toward the Cruiser. A male elephant ran ahead until it stood next to the vehicle. The elephant trailed its trunk on the hood, causing a loud thud followed by a swirling sound. Beatrice lifted her left arm and signaled with her hand. In response, the elephant's ears fanned back and forth, creating a gentle breeze that filled the Cruiser. Satisfied, the elephant turned back to join its family, and Beatrice veered the Cruiser toward a lake.

"That was one of the best moments of my life." Nyika confidently strode into Pamuzinda's thatched lodge. "Did you see those hippos in the water? Those beasts are massive."

"Man, you were crying in the backseat the entire trip." Derek laughed.

"That was joy, pure unadulterated joy at seeing nature in motion." Nyika grinned and joined the rest of group seated around the Lodge's fire pit.

"Did you guys see that cheetah move? The raw agility!" Makhosini dramatically waved his arms, causing the group to laugh hysterically.

"Would you like to take a walk?" Makhosini whispered to Danai. He reached for her hand, and the two snuck out of a side door.

"Nyika's right. This is the one of the most beautiful moments of my life." Danai stared at the indigo-blue sky embedded with endless stars.

"I know. I want to stay like this forever." He wrapped his arms around her and smiled in the dark.

"Forever's a long time to stand like this." Danai tickled him before pulling away and sprinting toward a maze of African apple trees. Like gushing water, her laughter drenched the safari park. Delirious with joy, Makhosini laughed and followed his girlfriend into the honey-scented maze.

"Let's eat, guys," Lillian glanced up at Makhosini and Danai walking back into the Lodge. "These ladies have to be home before nine p.m. or my brother-in-law's sending a search party!"

Beatrice returned through the side door. After a brief discussion on wildlife conservation and the importance of protecting endangered wildlife, she challenged the group to consider their role. "We all have a part to play in maintaining this ecosystem because we are part of the ecosystem," she explained. "It begins with small things like recycling and disposing our garbage appropriately rather than throwing it on the roadside." Before leaving for her evening tour, Beatrice led the visitors to a buffet of warm honey bread, roasted vegetables, and locally grown fruit.

A week later, Zimbabwe's Ministry of Education released the A-level results. Makhosini passed all four of his subjects with As. He started a new job as an intern at a local law firm. In the evenings he prepared for his SATs and began applying to universities.

"For us, the year 1991 began beautifully," Thulani confided in her mother.

Chapter Nineteen
"Come My Way"

"Danai!" A male voice broke into night's stillness. Danai's eyes searched the shadows and found the form emerging from the darkness.

"Oh, it's you! What are you doing here?" she asked.

The man grinned and leaned on the post of a street lamp. "Well, I was in the area and heard it through the grapevine that you're taking Wednesday night classes at Peter Birch." Peter Birch School of Art had opened its doors to give free lessons to five art students from Danai's high school. The students joined twenty artists who met weekly.

"How are you, Little Girl?" he smiled.

"I'm doing good but what are you doing here?"

"It's getting dark." His tall frame stepped out of the path of lamp light. "So, I figured someone should walk you home this late at night."

"What? It's only eight p.m., and this area is very safe. Besides, there are five of us." She pointed to the other girls walking with her. "We catch a taxi back to school together."

"Well, if you ladies wouldn't mind, I could escort you to the taxi depot." His familiar grin reappeared.

"That would be great!" the ever-friendly Sarah Carrington interrupted. Her eyelashes playfully fluttered as she ran her fingers through her blond curls. "Hi, I'm Sarah. That's Anesu, Elaine Wright, and Maidei Tatenda."

"Nice to meet you, ladies. I'm Derek Love." Derek laughed and joined the group.

Over the following weeks, Derek became the girls' regular escort after their art lessons. He was talkative, funny, and charming, and the girls looked forward to his company.

"Danai, where's Makhosini?" Derek asked one evening as they approached the taxi depot. He watched the other girls walk ahead. "He really should be the one walking you ladies on Wednesday nights."

"Derek, you know Makho is working, and at night he's busy preparing for his SAT." Since Baba cancelled their Saturday sessions four months ago, Danai rarely saw Makhosini.

"Yeah, I understand, but you're his girl, and you should be his priority. I believe any man in his right mind would make you his priority." Despite the disconcerting silence, Derek continued. "I hope I didn't offend you. I'm just curious because I hardly see you two together anymore."

"Derek, what exactly are you trying to say?" Danai asked with rising annoyance.

"Makhosini's my friend, but I was just wondering why he isn't taking care of you like he should be. He's out partying with the guys almost every weekend, but he can't take an hour out of his schedule to meet his girl and make sure you get back to school safely."

They walked the rest of the way in silence.

The following Wednesday, Derek arrived at Peter Birch carrying five yellow roses. He handed a rose to each girl.

"Derek, what is this?" Danai asked.

"A peace offering!" Derek declared. "I could tell I annoyed you last week. I treasure our friendship, and I don't want my comments to ruin it. I apologize, Danai." He handed the last rose to her. "So, are we cool?"

"Yeah, sure." She accepted his peace offering.

"Good. So, I'll say goodnight to you ladies." And with that, he left.

Danai woke up early Saturday morning to Miles leaning over her bed and grinning sheepishly.

"You've got a message, Princess. Makhosini called." Miles climbed onto the bed and lay next to Danai. "I told him you were busy snoring very loudly. He said when you finish snoring, I should ask you if you're free to go on a date with him." Miles giggled mischievously and bolted out of the room.

"I feel like I barely see you anymore." Danai followed Makhosini into Glamour House Spa. She hadn't seen him in two weeks, and Derek's comments still lingered in her mind.

"Yeah, I know. I'm still adjusting to this crazy work schedule." Makhosini paid for the couple's pedicure, and a wellness coordinator led the couple to their seats. "When I do have free time, I've been

130

running around getting my varsity applications in and helping my mother set up her new business." He chose the strawberry-butter scrub and settled his feet into a sparkling foot bath.

"But Makhosini, you barely call," Danai whispered. Her attendant forcefully squeezed her toes then massaged peppermint soufflé into her feet.

"I do call, but do you know how hard it is to get through to your school phone during the week?" Makhosini chuckled, and his attendant wrapped his feet in warm oil cloths. Derek had claimed Makhosini was out partying with the boys every weekend. The memory of Derek's words played with Danai's conscience, causing her to frown and shift uncomfortably.

"Is everything okay, babe?" Makhosini leaned forward and watched her. "Did something happen?"

Danai decided not to tell him about Derek's weekly visits or their conversation. She rested her head on the headrest and shut her eyes.

"There's this new exhibition tomorrow at Harare Art Gallery." Danai pulled a flyer from her purse. They walked out of Glamour House and strolled down First Street. "I really want you to come with me, Makhosini. It'll be nice."

"Ah babe, I can't. Tomorrow is the All-Hararians Soccer tournament." His boyish grin appeared as he ran his hand through his hair. "The boys and I already signed up to play."

"So, you still haven't told Makhosini?" Layla asked. The familiar sweet spicy aroma of Nando's garlic chicken filled her nostrils. Danai shook her head and glanced over her menu.

"When this place first opened two years ago, Daniel and I came here on a date." She smiled.

"And you were probably bored. Stop trying to change the subject." Layla rolled her eyes at the mention of the boy who had caused commotion in their lives. "Oh, look, there's Nyika and Derek!" Layla exclaimed.

Danai looked up. She hadn't seen Derek since the day he'd appeared carrying yellow roses. Nyika waved in their direction and rushed off to join the to-go line.

"Ladies, can I join you?" Derek approached their table.

"You're buying, right?" Layla joked.

"Of course," he chuckled and sat next to her. He casually draped his arm over Layla's shoulder, and Danai wondered if she'd overreacted.

"Hey, how was the All-Hararians Soccer tournament? Did you guys win?" Layla asked.

"We barely made it to the semifinals." Derek laughed. "I think we had more passion than play. You girls should've come. We were all there—me, Nyika, Will B., Makhosini, and Vanessa."

Danai grimaced. A vivid image of the tall girl with a cropped afro flickered through her mind. She'd seen Vanessa intimately laughing with the guys on more than one occasion.

"Only a friend!" Makhosini had described the chocolate beauty with endless legs and pouty lips. Wrapped in a body-hugging short purple dress and zebra-striped stilettos, the girl had walked away before Danai could ask any questions.

"Wait, who's Vanessa?" Layla's eyes danced with curiosity.

132

"Oh, Vanessa's Makhosini's friend. They're very close." Derek picked up his menu and refused to elaborate further. "Hey, Danai, didn't you say you were spending the night at Layla's? I'll drop you guys there."

"I feel like Derek's really shady," Layla muttered later that evening. "By the way, who is Vanessa?"

"What? You were the one who insisted Derek was cool." Danai flopped onto the bed next to her friend. "Well, I think he's nice. Besides, he's making more of an effort to hang out with me than Makhosini is."

"And that's exactly what bothers me." Layla lifted her head off her pillow. "Jealousy!"

"What?"

"White roses symbolize peace. Yellow roses mean jealousy." Layla sighed. "In the Victorian era, people sent yellow roses as a symbol of greed and jealousy." She rolled over, closed her eyes, and fell asleep.

Chapter Twenty
Going Up in Smoke

"You know, it's sad," Derek whispered, following Danai into Ricky's Ice Cream Shack. His eyes lingered over the sorbet bar before resting on Danai.

"What's sad, Derek?" she asked. After their lunch at Nando's, Derek had resumed his weekly visits. Despite Thulani and Layla's warnings, Danai welcomed his visits. To her, his presence became like water on dry ground.

"I've always liked you, and here I am in this romantic setting with you." He sighed. "But I keep reminding myself, she's my boy's girl. Why do things like this happen? The guy who doesn't deserve the girl gets her, and the guy who would love her right never wins." He placed his hand on his heart to imitate heartbreak.

"Derek, don't be silly." Danai laughed and settled in a booth by the window. A server appeared and scribbled their orders.

"No, seriously. I think it's so wonderful that you love Makhosini even though he's putting you through all this." Derek dipped his spoon into a bowl of ice cream.

"Derek, what are you trying to say?"

"I'm saying, not many women would accept Makhosini's past or him being so close with Vanessa." His spoon twirled between the cherries and chocolate chip ice cream. "Makhosini is a great friend though, and he's always been a wonderful father to Anashe."

"Wait, what? Who's Anashe?"

"Anashe is Makhosini's daughter." Dismayed at her reaction, Derek watched shock cross Danai's face. "I thought you knew. You mean Makhosini didn't tell you about his daughter?"

"What daughter?"

They sat staring at each other across half-empty bowls of cherry swirl and chocolate crisp.

"You really didn't know?" Derek broke the deafening silence. "I'm sorry, I thought you knew. Everyone does!"

"What daughter?" Danai struggled to breathe. Her voice sounded fragile.

"Danai, maybe you need to talk to Makhosini about this."

"No, enough is enough! I'm not talking to Makhosini about anything. First Vanessa, now a daughter. Tell your friend it's over. I'm done." She rose up and staggered toward the exit.

"Danai, wait." He rushed to pull her arm. "It's okay, Little Girl."

Tears trailed down Danai cheeks. She held tightly to the familiar stranger until she pushed him aside. Disorientated, she staggered out of Ricky's Ice Cream Shack.

The following morning, Derek appeared outside the Matamba residence.

"Danai, who's this boy that keeps coming here?" Mr. Matamba demanded. His eyes squinted at the morning sun rays and focused on a black Renault parked in the distance. "Why does he keep coming here, and where's Makhosini?"

"Oh, that's Derek. He's just a friend, Baba." She grabbed a sweater. Noting her father's disapproval, she mumbled, "Maybe he wants to speak to me about school."

She rushed past her father and joined Derek who patiently sat in his Renault.

"I hope you don't mind, but I came to make sure you are okay." Derek glanced at the man standing in the middle of the rose garden and swallowed nervously at the disapproval on the man's face. "Would you like to go for a drive and get some fresh air?" His eyes darted back to Mr. Matamba.

"Okay, but I have to come back soon."

They drove to a vast meadow.

"It's really beautiful here," Danai remarked, staring into the peaceful scenery. "Thank you for bringing me."

Derek's unexpected visit and the drive were a welcome distraction to the girl who had spent the night writhing on her bed in the dark.

"Danai, you probably don't want to hear this. But I apologize for my friend. Not all of us men are like that." He waited for her response,

136

but Danai remained silent. "I know you've just had your heart broken, but I'd like you to give me a chance to help mend it. I know this is sudden, and I'm willing to wait. I just wanted to let you know how I felt. Is that okay?" He leaned over and kissed her. Danai tasted the bitter wretchedness in her own heart and pulled away.

"Give me some time," she said once she recovered her senses. "I need to think about everything."

"Okay, I'll wait for you to sort out your feelings. I really do like you," he confessed.

"I like you, too, Derek," she shyly replied, "but I think you better take me home."

The black Renault reentered the Matambas' cobblestone courtyard. Derek strategically parked close to the gate to avoid Danai's father.

"Danai, I don't want to do anything in secrets and lies. And I know, even after all Makhosini's put you through, I wouldn't want to treat him the way he's treated you." His eyes flickered toward Mr. Matamba, who stood in the rose garden, glaring at him. "I think you should call Makhosini tonight and let him know that it's over and also about us."

Chapter Twenty-One
All Cried Out

"Are you crazy? Have you lost your mind?" Layla bellowed over the phone.

Danai wrapped her nightgown tightly around her body and sat on a chair at the console table. She hadn't called Makhosini that evening. Instead, she decided to phone Layla.

"But Layla, you don't understand. Derek told me that Makhosini's been lying about a daughter. Makhosini has a child, Layla!" Danai blurted. "And there's the whole Vanessa thing."

"What child? What Vanessa thing?" Layla's voice resonated through the telephone, causing the receiver to vibrate.

"Derek said. . ." Danai breathed out.

"Since when do you listen to what other people say without finding out the truth for yourself?" Layla sucked in her breath. "So, if someone told you I was a thief, you'd just believe them?"

"That's different, Layla. Stop interrupting me, okay?" Danai shouted. Her gaze shifted to Miles, who was sprawled on the couch pretending to read a comic book.

"Danai, I know you're upset right now." Her friend's voice took on a softer tone. "But are you sure you know what you're doing?"

"What do you mean?" she asked.

"Have you forgotten what happened with Daniel? Don't you remember how Daniel never asked your side of the story? He just went off and started dating someone else. Danai, you've just done the same thing to Makhosini. What were you thinking? Makhosini and Derek are friends!" she exclaimed.

Danai felt an uncomfortable tightness rushing through her stomach.

"I always knew that boy was brewing trouble," Layla muttered.

"Layla, I need to get off the phone." The discomfort in her stomach overflowed into her entire body. "I'll see you at school tomorrow."

"Okay, but don't think you can avoid me. I'm still your roommate." Layla hung up.

Surprisingly, Makhosini called repeatedly the following week. It became Thulani's job to tell him Danai could not come to the phone.

"Go upstairs, Thulani, and get your friend," Makhosini barked with rising annoyance. "Tell her to come to the phone booth or else I'm coming there." Thulani must've believed his threat because she rushed to her room and dragged Danai back to the student lounge.

139

"Hello," Danai mumbled.

"Hey you, are you okay? What's going on, Danai?" Makhosini's voice seeped through the receiver. "I've called several times. Speak to me. What's going on, babe? Why have you been ignoring me?"

"Makhosini, who is Anashe?" Danai demanded. An eternity of silence passed between them.

"Anashe is my daughter," he mumbled. The softness in his voice drastically contrasted with Danai's agitation.

"What? Your daughter!" she yelled, and her body shook bitterly. "What daughter, Makhosini? We've been together for over a year and somehow you forgot to tell me you have a daughter?" Danai could hear Makhosini speaking, but she was too unraveled to understand a word he said.

"So does this mean you are married?" Danai hissed. With a few exceptions, everyone she knew who had a child was married.

"No, Danai, I'm not married!" Makhosini shouted.

"I don't believe you." She groaned and stared at Thulani's bewildered expression. With her hand covering her mouth, Thulani staggered backwards until she fell onto a potted plant.

"Why should I believe you? I don't believe anything you have to say," Danai shouted.

"Danai, I wanted to tell you about Anashe," Makhosini stuttered. "I was going to, but I was afraid you'd leave me. I am sorry."

"Everyone knew. Everyone, except me! Imagine that! Now I'm everyone's fool, right?" She moaned in anguish. The phone slid from her fingers, hit the floor, and broke.

Layla called an emergency meeting in Thulani's room. The girls split their attention between consoling their friend and arguing about Makhosini's actions. Danai sat in silence staring at the naked wall. Eventually she stopped listening to her bickering friends and fell asleep on Thulani's bed.

Chapter Twenty-Two
Ain't Nothing Changed

"Come on, Daddy." The passenger door of a silver Mercedes swung open. A little girl hopped out. Her laughter filled the school parking lot. The girl adjusted her multicolored dress and turned to a man stepping out of the car's driver seat.

"Come on, let's walk fast," she demanded. Without waiting for the man striding behind her, the girl ran toward a pond.

"Look, Daddy, they got fishes." She peered into clear waters and ran her fingers through the swirling waters. "Look, they got yellow fishes and green fishes, Daddy."

"Hey, isn't that Makhosini?" Layla pointed toward the pond next to the school parking lot. Surprised, Thulani and Danai turned and gaped in dismay. Makhosini walked to the pond and knelt next to the little girl. The two engaged in a lengthy discussion on ponds and fish.

142

Satisfied, the girl placed her hand in her father's hand, and the two walked toward the girls. Stunned at the likeness between father and daughter, the girls gasped. With exact facial features, Anashe looked like a miniature female Makhosini.

"Hi, my name is Sugarbaby, and this is my daddy." The little girl stopped in front of the girls.

"Hi," Layla and Thulani choked in unison.

"You must be Anashe!" Layla exclaimed.

"No," the girl objected, "I'm Sugarbaby." She looked at her father, seeking his affirmation. Seeing him nod, the little girl continued, "We come to play. Me and my daddy."

"What are you doing, Makhosini?" Layla's eyes darted toward Danai, who looked flabbergasted.

"I hope you don't mind, but I really wanted you to meet my daughter," Makhosini explained. His eyes remained on Thulani, while avoiding Danai's piecing gaze. "I should have introduced her sooner."

"How old are you?" Thulani scrutinized the doll-like girl.

"I'm four years old. That's this much." Anashe showed off four tiny fingers then tilted her head and asked Thulani, "How old are you?"

Makhosini picked up his daughter.

"Daddy, did they say we can we stay and play?" Sugarbaby whispered. Makhosini looked at Danai and nodded. Sugar screamed in glee and raced ahead of the group. Ripe with curiosity, the child explored the girls' boarding school, stopping to ask questions about everything she laid her eyes on.

"Who lives in there?" Sugar pointed at a vacant classroom. "Whose dogs are they? Can I pat them?" Without waiting for an answer, she reached into the wire fence and stroked Mr. Ritchie's greyhounds. Determined to satisfy her curiosity, Sugar ran into the auditorium and climbed onto a low seat. Her tiny fingers trailed the edge of a grand piano before plonking on the keys.

"This is something new, a novelty for her. She gets excited about new experiences," Makhosini apologetically explained. His eyes nervously flickered toward Danai, who had remained silent since his arrival.

"How have you been?" he asked her.

"Why don't we walk to the racquetball courts?" Thulani suggested. She glanced at a group of students who'd stopped their activities and gathered to watch. "Too many prying eyes here."

"Daddy, I think I need to potty," Sugar whispered as they neared the racquetball courts. She grabbed Layla's hand. "Auntie, I think I have to go. Can you take me?"

"Danai, why don't you go with her?" Layla turned toward her best friend.

"What? Why me?" Danai mumbled.

"I think you should go with her." Layla sounded like a mother. Sugar released Layla's hand and clutched onto Danai's arm. Oblivious to the older girl's discomfort, Sugar patiently waited for Danai to lead the way.

"Is this where you live?" Sugar's tiny fingers glided over Danai's study table. "Thank you for taking me to the toilet, Auntie." Torn between liking the little girl and resenting Makhosini's deception, Danai settled onto a chair and quietly observed Sugar playing on her bed.

"Is this yours?" Sugar asked and pointed to a cup created with layers of intertwined copper wire. Her fingers stroked the colorful silk butterflies attached to the cup. "It's very pretty."

"I made it in drawing class." Danai explained. She carefully placed the copper cup into the little girl's hands.

"Really, you are a really good maker." Sugar's eyes danced in appreciation, and Danai giggled in amusement.

"You can have it." Danai smiled.

"Really?" Sugar's face exploded with joy. "Thank you, Auntie Danai. I'll keep it good, and I won't even drop it," she promised.

"I think your daddy's still with my friends. They're meeting us at the snack shop." With the four-year old's curiosity satisfied, Danai led Sugar out of Sable dorm. They headed to the Snack Canteen Kiosk.

"Auntie Danai, are you my daddy's girlfriend?" Sugar licked the sherbet off her sugar-coated fingers as she sat next to Danai on the grass outside the kiosk waiting for Makhosini.

"Yes."

"Do you love my daddy?"

"I don't know," Danai muttered and watched sadness trail down Sugar's face. "I mean, sometimes I do love him, but sometimes I'm not sure," she explained and fed Sugarbaby a scoop of frozen yogurt.

"I love him, too!" Sugar shouted in joy. "I love him this much." To Danai's dismay, Sugar rose to her feet, stretched her arms as wide as she could, and began dancing in circles while singing, "Daddy's got a girlfriend. Daddy's got a girlfriend."

"That girl is too full of life." Layla giggled, "Makhosini's talking to Thulani at the racquetball courts. They're on their way."

145

When Makhosini arrived, Sugar waved bye to the girls and obediently ran to the car. She hopped into the passenger seat and quietly waited for her father.

"At least now we know what's been keeping you so busy." Thulani shook her head at Makhosini before walking back to her dorm room.

"Danai, do you have some time?" Makhosini moved toward Danai. "Can we talk?"

"I don't know. I'm not sure I'm ready to talk." She glanced at Thulani and Layla walking away in the distance. "I'm not even sure I want to talk to you about anything."

"I know." He inhaled and ran his fingers through his hair. "I should have told you the truth about Anashe from the beginning. I really messed up, and nothing I can say will ever change that. I'm sorry, Danai. Can we sit and talk please?"

"You hurt me," Danai moaned. "How can I ever trust you again?" She slowly walked through the secluded parking lot.

"Danai?" he whimpered, following her. "Will you at least listen to me?"

"Where's Anashe's mother?"

"What?" Makhosini's gaze darted toward his daughter. "I don't know. We haven't seen or heard from her since the day Anashe was born." They both stared at the little girl peering at them from the passenger seat.

"Danai, please forgive me?" he asked as they neared his car.

"I don't know if I can forgive you." The words echoed throughout the school parking lot, and Sugar watched sadness trail down her father's face, and Auntie Danai walk away. Her father got into the car, and they drove back home.

"What's going on? It's been two days since you came home that you've been moping around in your room." Mrs. Matamba entered her daughter's bedroom.

"A strange illness," the school nurse had said when she called to urge Danai's mother to come and pick up her daughter. Mrs. Matamba had arrived an hour later. She'd briefly spoken to the dorm matron and Thulani before taking her daughter home. Surprisingly, Danai's parents didn't make an issue of their daughter coming home in the middle of the week.

"Why don't you come and help me with the preparations for your father's surprise birthday party? Remember, it's tonight."

Mother and daughter drove to a shanty bottle store in Chitungwiza and purchased several crates of beer and soft drinks. While Mrs. Matamba watched the men loading the crates onto her pickup truck, Danai sat in the passenger seat and wept into a stack of tissues. After Chitungwiza, they headed to Auntie Chantelle's bakery in Glendale. Auntie Chantelle and Danai's mother sat in the tiny shop, sipping tea while Danai carried Baba's massive birthday cake to their car. With each step, fresh tears streamed down her face and soaked into the cake's strawberry-vanilla icing.

"Eeh, happy birthday. You're fifty years old now. You've lived half a century," Uncle Tadiwa, Mr. Matamba's younger brother, joked and entered the Matamba residence. "Ha, you're really an old man. You'll probably need this now." He pulled out an old walking stick and handed it to Mr. Matamba. The other guests burst into laughter.

Lively chatter filled the house as thirty guests, including Uncle Farai and his family and Danai's aunts and their families celebrated Mr. Matamba's fiftieth birthday. Uncle Tadiwa retold stories of their childhood growing up in the rural area and the struggles and successes that had marked Mr. Matamba's journey through life. Danai watched her father during the impromptu speech. He looked tired but was smiling with genuine appreciation. As Danai listened to Uncle Tadiwa, her respect for Baba grew. Between their relatives' unrehearsed speeches and helping her mother, Danai found herself laughing for the first time in days.

"Are you feeling better now?" Mrs. Matamba asked after the last guest left.

"Yes, I think so," Danai whispered. She flopped onto the garden couch and laid her head in the warmth of her mother's lap. "I think I'm going to be okay, Mama." They both stared at endless stars embedded in a velvety night sky. In the quiet evening, her mother seemed to instinctively know all the things Danai hadn't told her.

"Your cousin's having another baby." Mrs. Matamba stared at the brightest star. Her voice strained under the weight of her announcement. "Monique's pregnant again!"

"What?" Danai lifted her head and stared at her mother. "I thought she and Dumelo got divorced. Didn't she say she was leaving him and going back to school?"

"That's what we all thought," Mrs. Matamba sighed. "It's a different guy this time. His name is Innocence. Your Auntie Chastity is speechless! She's devastated."

"Mama, why did Aunty Chastity leave Monique at our house that night?"

"I don't know why she abandoned that child, but our mother was that way too," Mrs. Matamba muttered. She clutched her daughter closely to her bosom until the two fell asleep in the garden.

Chapter Twenty-Three
River Flowing Beneath

"What is this?" Layla and Danai barged into Thulani's room. Dumbfounded, they stared at a huge bouquet of flowers next to Thulani's desk. The elaborate flower arrangement looked as tall as their petite friend.

"And that?" Danai pointed to a triple-layered cherry and chocolate mousse cake on Thulani's desk.

"Happy anniversary. Giles and Thulani—us forever," Danai read the inscription aloud.

"It's our two-year anniversary." Thulani blushed and removed a silk ribbon from a gift box. Her friends sighed in awe as Thulani pulled out a collection of novels by her favorite authors.

"Wait, so what did you get him?' Layla asked.

"Nothing!" Thulani's musical voice confessed. "I forgot."

Her friends broke into tumultuous laughter and fell onto her bed.

"That's terrible, Thulani. Giles is such a good boyfriend. If you can't be a good girlfriend, then hand him over. We'll be better girlfriends to him," Layla teased.

"Yes, we'd send him sweet candy cake for our anniversary." Danai joined her friend's humor. "And we'd make him chocolate coated strawberries for his birthday."

"Never!" Thulani protested, laughing.

During her third year of high school, Thulani had joined the school's debating club. At the first interschool debate, she listened diligently and sat wide-eyed as a scruffy boy defended his stance on the benefits of merging all fifty-four African countries into one nation. An enthusiastic visionary who was the product of pan-African parents, eighteen-year-old Giles meticulously asserted his argument. Ultimately, he'd lost the debate but won Thulani's attention. Shy Thulani, who habitually stood in the background and rarely spoke, approached Giles.

"I want to get to know you," she whispered into his ear. And that's how they met. What began as a random encounter rapidly blossomed into an enduring two-year romance.

"Ladies, I'm telling you, the best way to get over past people is to go out and meet new people. That's what happened to me when I joined that debate club." Thulani pulled her friends off her bed. After her first meeting with Giles, Thulani quit the debate team and joined Sisters Book Club.

"It's not an official school club, but being a member of Sisters Book Club has redefined my life," Thulani explained. "Come with me and you'll see."

Comprised of fifteen members, Sisters Book Club met once a week in an abandoned study room. The club members were as diverse and unique as the books they read. On Danai's first evening visiting the book club, a chubby, plain-faced white girl stood up. In the stillness of a cool evening, the girl spoke into the night and recited Maya Angelou's "Phenomenal Woman." Her voice evoked, energized, and tantalized her listeners until each member rose from their seats and joined in the recital. Walls vibrated, and the ground shook under the unified chant of the sisters. Intrigued, Danai sat in a corner with her mouth open wide.

"Everything in me is hungry to know about Zora Neale Hurston during the Harlem Renaissance," Danai told Thulani as they strolled back to their dorm room.

"Girl, don't you want to know what happened to Wole Soyinka's Lion and his Jewel?" Thulani laughed into the night.

A week later, Danai signed up as Sisters Book Club's sixteenth member. In the solace of their tiny meeting room, the sisters drank hot chocolate, listened to Pavarotti, and argued about Agatha Christie's latest suspect. The books the girls read overflowed into their personal lives.

"It's funny, when I go home on the weekends, I'm spending more time with Mbuya and my parents and asking questions about their own lives," Danai confided in Layla. She didn't forget Makhosini. She quietly packed him in the secret place of her hidden depths.

"Hey, Danai, I've been looking everywhere for you." A first-year student rushed into the meeting. The clumsy girl meandered between girls seated on randomly placed mats. "You have a phone call. I think it's important," she said.

Danai rose from her floor pillow and followed the girl back to the school phone booth. She picked up the receiver. "Hello."

"Why haven't you called me back? I've called you several times," the caller demanded.

"Derek?"

"Yes, Danai, it's me. Why haven't you called me back?"

"I've been busy," she lied, glancing at the other students in the lounge. She hadn't seen Derek in the month following their kiss. Danai wasn't sure why she felt reluctant to see him, but she'd avoided him.

"I understand you're busy, but we need to talk." Derek's frustration seeped through the phone.

"No, Derek," Danai breathed. "I made a mistake, and I just want to forget what happened."

"What are you saying?" Derek yelled in desperation. "You know I love you, but you are talking about forgetting me!"

"Derek, you barely know me. I'm tired, and I really have to go."

"What about Makhosini?" Derek's words pierced through the phone, and Danai stopped breathing. Her grip tightened around the receiver.

"What *about* Makho?" she asked.

"Does Makhosini know about us?" His question sounded like a threat. "Should I tell him?"

"Derek, this is enough. Please stop and leave me alone." She hung up the phone.

A week after his disconcerting phone call, Derek showed up at the girls' boarding school.

"Hey, Danai, there's some guy here to see you," a first-year student shouted. Thulani, Layla, and Danai followed the student back to the school car parking lot and found Derek standing by his black Renault.

"Derek, what are you doing here?" Danai asked.

"We need to talk, Danai." He reached into his passenger seat and pulled out a bouquet of purple roses.

"I keep telling you that I don't want to talk. Why are you here?" Danai asked. She resented him for the way she'd found out about Anashe. It had been Makhosini who'd lied, but she distrusted Derek's motives.

"You've treated me unfairly, and I'm not leaving until we sit down and talk." He moved closer to the girls.

"Whatever happened between Danai and you is over, Derek." Thulani's soft voice interrupted their conversation. "You should accept that and just let go."

"Stay out of this, Thulani," Derek shouted. "Where were you when I was taking your friend out and trying to be there for her? Why didn't you give your two cents advice back then, huh? And you—" He swerved around and glared at Layla. "You weren't protesting when I paid for your meal at Nando's."

"What does that have to do with anything?" Layla glared back at Derek. "The girl doesn't want to be with you, and she's asking you to leave. You know what, I'm done talking." Layla abruptly turned and headed to Mrs. Moffat's suite. Uncertain of Layla's intentions, Thulani and Danai followed in pursuit of their friend.

"Mrs. Moffat, he's my cousin." Layla theatrically explained to their head matron. "I think he's developed a serious infatuation for Danai. I keep telling him that Danai is a good girl. You know, she just wants to finish high school quietly and start dating after high school, but he keeps calling, and now he's here."

"He's your cousin?" Mrs. Moffat's aging blue eyes scrutinized the three girls.

"Yes. I thought of calling my father," Layla added. She watched Mrs. Moffat's eyelids flicker nervously at the mention of Dr. Njeke. "I would call my father about this problem with my *cousin,* but I felt that as head matron you would want to handle this situation yourself."

Mrs. Moffat knew better than to believe Layla's story. However, the elderly matron clearly understood an unwanted stranger had entered her territory. Fuming at the stranger's insolence, Mrs. Moffat emerged from her suite and headed to the school parking lot. The stern-faced matron gave Derek an extensive lecture on the dangers of leading innocent girls astray. With her purple-tinted gray wig falling off, she grabbed Derek by the collar and forcefully escorted him back to his car. "Leave school grounds at once!" she ordered.

After his encounter with Mrs. Moffat, Derek stopped calling and seemingly disappeared into the past.

Chapter Twenty-Four
You, Me, and Him

"Lilly, we haven't gone out forever. Let's go out tonight," Danai pleaded. "I feel like dancing."

Ignoring her niece's pouting lips, Lillian walked past Danai and shut her bedroom door.

"Lilly, I really want to go to this party," Danai begged with exaggerated agony. "You know everyone's saying Taka's throwing the party of the year!"

"Danai, every party is the party of the year." Lillian came back out of her bedroom wearing her favorite floral pajamas. "Tonight I just want to stay home and relax on this couch." She lazily flopped onto the couch and turned on the TV. "Why don't you call Makhosini? Maybe he could come here and pick you up."

"I already tried that. I called his house, but he's not there," Danai lied. In truth, she was trying to avoid Derek. "I think the guys already left and went to a different party."

"So, are you two back together?" Lilly tried to make sense of the confusion.

"I don't know." Danai turned away. Since his visit with Sugar, Makhosini had become a frequent visitor at Danai's boarding school. When he arrived with the bubbly Sugarbaby in tow, the girls welcomed their visits. More often, though, Makhosini came alone. He talked, and Danai argued. He listened and then quietly swore in frustration. They took long walks and occasionally laughed together. The world watched as Makhosini and Danai would sit in silence for hours without uttering a word.

"I don't know if we are starting again or beginning to end," Danai mumbled.

"Well, get ready anyway." Lilly gulped a spoonful of ice cream and shook her head. "Godfrey's planning on stopping here. It's almost midnight, but I'll persuade him to go with you, so stop bothering me."

"What happened to 'life is now' Lilly?" Danai laughed gleefully and ran to Lilly's bedroom.

"Today life is right here," Lillian shouted, stretching out her legs. "On this couch, eating rum and raisin ice cream and watching TV."

Taka Musikwa's parents had taken a short trip out of town. Unbeknownst to them, their son used their absence as an opportunity to throw what was now rumored to be the party of the year. Taka's home, a large private estate located in the heart of Borrowdale Brook, became the venue for his rebellion. Cars lined up for miles on the streets surrounding the estate. Crowds of loud people dressed to party filled the street and woke the sleeping suburb. Despite Godfrey's connections, it took him and Danai over an hour before they were admitted through Taka's brass gates.

Filled with growing anticipation, Danai followed Godfrey into the crowded gardens. She stopped to talk to a girl from her high school and realized she had lost sight of Godfrey.

"I think they're in the house," the pretty girl explained. "I saw him follow Taka in earlier."

"Manheru Mbuya." Danai walked into the kitchen and greeted an elderly housekeeper.

"No one is allowed in the house, sisi," the woman responded.

"I'm sorry to walk in the house, but I'm looking for Godfrey." She described Godfrey to the elderly housekeeper. "I need to find him, or I won't be able to get home. I heard he came in here with Taka."

The woman looked at her doubtfully before pointing to a secluded passageway.

"Godfrey!" Danai shouted. She recognized his blond curls at the entrance of a room. "I've been looking for you everywhere. What are you doing here?"

"Danai, go and wait for me in the car!" Godfrey tried to block her view into the room while he searched his pockets for the car keys.

"What's going on, Godfrey?" Danai pushed past him and stepped into a large lounge. She glanced at three panic-stricken dealers standing near a couch. Taka frantically paced the room. Everyone's eyes were focused on something at the center of the room. Ignoring Godfrey's plea, Danai pushed farther to view the object of their attention. Derek

158

sat slouched on the floor. Despite his elegant outfit, Derek looked disheveled and confused. In his left hand he held a beer bottle. Next to him lay a small bottle of pills.

"He tried killing himself," one dealer explained, shoving a crumpled piece of paper into Danai's hand. Forcing her eyes away from Derek, Danai read the note. In scribble, Derek had written the details of the events that had occurred between them.

"Why couldn't you love me?" his letter concluded. Stupefied, she dropped onto the cold marble floor. When Danai looked up, all eyes were now focused on her. She rose up in panic and turned to run away.

"What did you do, Danai?" Makhosini's iron grip tightened around her wrist. His eyes remained on Derek while his hushed tone demanded, "What did you do, Danai?"

"Get this guy out of my house." Taka's frustration exploded. His arms wildly flailed.

"Calm down, man," a dealer screamed. "You need to chill. Don't you see him crying?"

"No, I'm not calming down. If my parents find out about this, I'm dead meat!" Taka insisted. His agitation resonated throughout the house. "Guys, you gotta go. All of you!"

"Danai, why didn't you love me?" Derek mumbled from the hard floor. He stared at the girl who had rejected him.

"I'm sorry, Derek," she whimpered. Salty tears intermixed with bitter makeup seeped into her mouth. She slowly walked toward Derek. In shock, Makhosini watched his girlfriend kneel next to the crying boy slouched on the floor.

"I never meant to hurt you," she moaned. Between them lay the bottle of pills and the now-empty beer bottle.

"You should have loved me," Derek's feeble voice whispered. His sadness filled the space separating them. Through her veil of tears, Danai glanced up. Nyika now stood next to Makhosini. Both boys were staring in disbelief.

"No, don't call the police." Taka's voice screeched at the dealer standing next to him. "Just get these people out of here. Use that side door so nobody will see you leave."

Derek lifted himself up and stumbled onto his feet. He staggered past Nyika and Makhosini. Ignoring Taka's protests, Derek walked down the dark passageway and out of the main door.

"Danai," Godfrey whispered. She felt his gentle hand on her back. "It's time to go home."

Met by the explosive blast of music and an occasional curious stare, Godfrey clung to Danai's hand and led their way out of the brass gates. Oblivious to the events that had taken place in the house, the invigorated party crowd danced, and Taka's party continued.

"Are you okay?" Godfrey asked. "Danai, what happened between you and Derek?"

Danai opened her mouth to speak, but she couldn't. Godfrey allowed his head to fall onto the cold steering wheel. An eternity passed as Godfrey's head remained buried on the steadiness of the wheel.

"A few months ago, Derek's father left their home. He didn't say where he was going or why he was leaving. His father woke up one morning and simply walked out." Godfrey lifted his head and spoke

160

into the silence. They both stared at the growing crowd clamoring outside the brass gates. Desperate to enter the party, the crowd pushed in.

"That man grabbed the family's wealth and left behind a hungry family and a stack of bills. Derek later discovered his father had moved into a new house with a second wife. What's crazy is when we were growing up, Derek was always the wealthiest kid, and now overnight it's all disappeared. Derek and his siblings must now fend for themselves. He's the eldest of eight children, and all the responsibility for their family has fallen on him." Godfrey's voice sounded soft yet shaky. As he spoke, Danai could feel the brokenness in Godfrey's heart. "Derek's mother has been sick for a year. Yesterday, Derek drove her to the hospital. She was admitted to Parirenyatwa Hospital, and the doctors diagnosed her with AIDS." He pulled the crumpled letter out of Danai's hand and tore it into tiny pieces.

Delirious with confusion, Makhosini walked out of the brass gates. He pushed his way through the crowd until he saw Godfrey's Mazda. Godfrey stepped out of his car and followed Makhosini to a secluded area in the distance. The boys argued until Makhosini folded over and vomited into the muddy ground, then repeatedly retched. Horrified, Godfrey stopped arguing and stood in silence. After a brief hesitation, Godfrey turned away and headed back to his car.

"Danai, Makhosini will take you home." He reached into the backseat and grabbed a jacket. "I need to go to hospital and make sure Derek's okay." He shot a warning look at Makhosini, who reluctantly entered the driver's seat. Between Makhosini's icy silence and Danai's uninhibited crying, their already fragile world shattered into pieces.

Mr. Matamba sat under the silver moonlight in the garden. He relaxed among a sea of roses, enjoying the solace of his favorite pastime. Using an outdoor side lamp, he read a news article while sipping on a glass of Cognac.

A yellow Mazda trailed onto the cobblestone court. Surprised by the unexpected intrusion, Baba looked up. He watched his daughter and Makhosini get out of the car. Danai mumbled a greeting and ran into their home.

Makhosini entered the rose garden and sat down in the seat opposite Danai's father. Makhosini's expression remained emotionless as he spoke in a barely audible voice. From her hiding place, Danai watched her father's expression slowly transform from confusion to shock. Baba's gaze fell to the ground before he buried his head in his hands. Makhosini slowly rose from his seat, staggered back to his car, and drove off. In panic, Danai rushed to her room and buried herself under the blankets. Beneath the bedcovers, she lay wide awake until dawn eventually appeared.

"Sisi, why are you crying?" Miles strode into his sister's room. He climbed onto her bed and lay next to her.

"Who says I'm crying?" Danai asked between sniffles.

"I could hear you crying the whole night," he whispered. "You shouldn't be sad. What's wrong, Danai?" He wrapped his arms around his sister.

Danai told Miles about Derek and the events at Taka's party.

"Sisi, don't cry anymore. I don't think it was your fault," the twelve-year-old concluded. "I mean, who would try to die for you?" he teased, holding his sister closer. "I think maybe there are things—like lots of things—happening in his life, and he didn't know what to do, so he tried killing himself. But maybe it's not because of you."

Miles' reasoning reminded Danai of Godfrey's words. She held onto her brother and wept into his shoulder.

"You have a call." Mr. Chris stuck his head through the door. He stared in confusion at the siblings before handing Danai the cordless phone.

"Hello, are you okay?" Lillian asked. "Derek's doing better. The doctors say he'll probably be discharged home tomorrow."

Danai felt tears of relief rolling down her cheeks. She lay back down on the bed and fell asleep in Miles' arms.

"Oh, good, you're here, you made it." Mr. Matamba said.

It was the following morning. Makhosini walked into the dining room, his cold gaze rested on Danai, who sat huddled by a corner of the dinner table. She stared at the untouched plate of food in front of her.

"How is your friend doing today?" Mr. Matamba asked Makhosini, glancing at his daughter. "Have you had a chance to speak to him?"

"Yes, I went to the hospital yesterday." Makhosini settled into a chair opposite Danai. "He says he's fine, but he doesn't remember anything." He shot an accusing look at Danai, who quickly looked back down at her plate to avoid his gaze.

"The hospital discharged him early this morning after the twenty-four-hour observation," Makhosini explained. Sadness filled his wary gaze. "Derek's mother is still in the hospital, so I'm going there after here."

"Yes, yes." Mr. Matamba picked up a napkin and wiped the sweat gathering on his forehead. "We'll go with you."

Danai and Miles followed Mr. Matamba and Makhosini though Parirenyatwa Hospital and entered a secluded ward.

"I guess we're a little early," Mr. Matamba surveyed the isolated ward.

"Hello, I'm a distant relative of the family," a friendly middle-aged lady standing at the room's entrance introduced herself. Derek and Will B. sat in a corner of the room.

"How are you doing? Are you okay, Derek?" Mr. Matamba asked. He embraced the boy. "Never do that again. Your life is too precious, son."

Derek's mother lay propped up by two pillows. Despite her futile attempts to smile and appear well, she looked thin and haggard. Her eyes and cheeks were notably sunken, and her frail body winced with every movement. Mr. Matamba pulled a chair and sat beside her bed. He introduced himself as the father of Derek's friend. The two adults exchanged traditional greetings and engaged in small talk until both felt comfortable enough to sit in silence.

"I guess we came a little early," Mr. Matamba commented, noting the lack of family and friends visiting the patient.

"You're not early or late. Our relatives won't be coming." Derek's mother smiled wryly. With great effort, she moved from her side and sat up in the bed. "My husband left with the money. Our relatives followed the money. No one else is coming."

Danai glanced at Derek and watched the anger burning in his eyes. Mr. Matamba saw it too and changed the subject. He introduced his children. Miles stepped forward and respectfully greeted Derek's mother.

"It's good to finally meet you, Danai." Derek's mother's eyes overflowed with genuine warmth. "Are you okay?" she asked.

Avoiding the woman's gaze, Danai nodded.

At Baba's insistence, the boys left the room and went to a nearby canteen. They later returned carrying bottles of Fanta and Coca-Cola, sausage rolls, and meat pies. The group ate while the adults continued to sit in silence.

"Come closer, Danai," Derek's mother called the broken girl to her bedside.

"Yes, Auntie." Danai approached the bed.

"Can you see how I am?" Derek's mother gently took Danai's hand in hers.

"Yes, Auntie," the anguished girl mumbled.

"I need my son, Danai," she winced in pain. Her sorrow-filled eyes flickered in the direction of her grief-stricken son. "I need my son."

A surge of remorse filled Danai's heart. Her watering eyes fell to the floor. "I'm sorry, Auntie," Danai whimpered. She looked up at Derek and wept.

"I know, Danai, I know." Derek's mother patted Danai's hand before releasing it. "Thank you for coming to see me. Visitors are truly a treasure to a sick person." Derek's mother smiled in Miles' direction before she rested her head back on the pillows and fell asleep.

Chapter Twenty-Five
Right Back to You

Who can ever forget June winters? Marked with frost-sprinkled mornings and bitter freezing nights, Zimbabwe's winters are brutal. At dawn, the sky transforms herself into a silvery gray tent. When the sun does appear, June's biting wind constantly announces winter's arrival.

"Our family month," Mrs. Matamba described the excruciating period when families locked themselves indoors. With Miles' assistance, she redecorated the house one room at a time. Seeking the warmth of the fireplace, Mbuya sat in the living room and entertained whichever relative chose to visit that day. Mr. Matamba hid in the sanctuary of his study and worked from home. Mr. Chris used the chilly month to unveil his scrumptious new recipes. Today the succulent smell of roasting lamb, baking sweet potatoes, and warm apple pie filled the Matamba residence.

"Danai." Baba's voice echoed throughout the house, invading the soft sounds of Hugh Masekela. "Danai?"

"Yes, Baba." Danai laid down the novel she was reading. "I'm coming, Baba."

Mr. Matamba stood at the main entrance amidst the distinct chatter of male voices. Two young men stood with Baba. Their conversation ended when Danai walked into the lounge.

"Ah, Danai, Makhosini is here with. . . mmm. . .." Her father looked baffled.

"Nyika, sir," Nyika confidently announced.

"Ah, yes, Nyika. I still have some work to finish, so I'll leave you young people." Her father headed back toward his study. "Danai, don't forget, it's almost time for lunch."

"Nice crib!" Nyika surveyed the lounge with appreciation. He introduced himself to Mbuya and flopped on the sofa near her armchair. The two promptly embarked on an engaging conversation.

"Hi, Danai." Makhosini turned to the girl staring at him in bewilderment. "How have you been?"

"I'm doing fine," she mumbled.

"Would you like to take a walk?" He smiled at the uncertainty in her gaze.

Confused by his sudden appearance, Danai walked to her room and returned with her sweater and sneakers.

"I haven't seen you around lately." Makhosini adjusted his coat and followed Danai out of the main door. "You didn't come to Lillian's birthday party." It had been two months since Lilly's birthday, and Danai had stuck to her resolve to let Makhosini go. She glanced up at her brother peeking through a side window and strode further from the house.

"You were missed." Makhosini chuckled.

"By who?" Danai asked, wrapping her arms around her waist against the crisp breeze.

"Everyone," he grinned.

"I sincerely doubt that." She smiled and slowed her pace. In the months following Derek's incident, Makhosini had avoided Danai. Whenever she'd appeared where he was, he had ignored her. "I got tired of seeing that scowl on your face every time we happened to be at the same place."

"Am I still scowling?" he mused.

"A little." She jokingly pointed at the side of his mouth.

"Maybe you give up too easily," Makhosini teased.

"Some things are too hard." She stopped walking and asked, "Makhosini, why are you here?"

The night when Derek had stepped out of the darkness at Peter Birch, Danai never imagined things would end with them weeping on a stranger's floor. She still agonized over the memory of Derek's pain and the brokenness she'd seen in Makhosini's eyes, but she was hurting, too. On that night, she'd seen Makhosini's hurt and anguish. Danai had desperately gone to the places she knew Makhosini would be and tried telling him how sorry she was, but her efforts were met with icy indifference.

"Some things are just too hard," she repeated, groaning at the memory. The wind dispassionately swept through her dress, making her shiver. "I better go back to the house. It's almost lunch time, and my parents are waiting."

"Can I come back tomorrow?" Makhosini opened the door. They both reentered the warmth of the Matamba home. "There's somewhere I'd like to take you, but it would be early, like six a.m. Will you come?"

"I'm not sure. I'll have to ask Baba," she replied.

Makhosini's car appeared on the cobblestone courtyard early the following morning. The Matambas' main door swung open, and Miles staggered past him toward the car. Without a word, the twelve-year-old rolled into the backseat and fell back into a deep sleep.

"Baba said I could only go if Miles came with me," Danai explained. She covered her brother with a blanket and settled into the passenger seat.

They drove north then veered onto a familiar dirt road. "A Peace of Heaven" declared a withered sign at the end of a wooden bridge. Dawn hadn't fully unveiled herself, but the brilliant moonlight stroked everything in sight, making the landscape easily visible. Leaving Miles sleeping in the backseat, Danai stepped out of the car and followed Makhosini toward the lake.

"It's beautiful here, even in the darkness of a winter morning," Danai murmured, surveying the glistening dew-glazed landscape. She wrapped her sweater tighter to shield out the cutting wind. "Makhosini, why did you bring me here?"

"Do you remember the first time we came here?" Makhosini walked further into paradise. "That day, I felt like I could talk to you about anything. I wanted to tell you everything." He slowed his pace and stared into the distance.

Danai's chest tightened. Did Makhosini intend to break up with her in the very paradise they began?

"Danai, why did you do it?" Makhosini asked and turned to her.

Confronted by the weight of his question, Danai's legs weakened. "I don't know, Makho." She wrapped her arms against her chest and glanced down at her trembling fingers. "I guess I just didn't trust us."

"What do you mean?" he asked.

"When we started, you were dating Melissa, and I was with Daniel. And I guess at the back of my mind, I was always thinking that if you treated her that way, why wouldn't you do the same to me?"

"But I never did that to you," Makhosini whispered into the dark. "Derek was my friend, Danai." He groaned and stared at the girl in the shadows. She slowly crumpled onto the moist grass. "You were my girl. I trusted you, and the whole time you were messing around with my boy." His anguish soaked into the atmosphere.

"Makhosini, I'm sorry I cheated on you. I'm sorry I hurt you." Tears trailed down Danai's cheeks. A lone leaf grazed her cheek while the biting wind attempted to steal her words.

"You hurt me." Makhosini sobbed.

"I know. I hurt you, and now I don't know what to do." Separated by pain, an eternity passed as Makhosini and Danai wept in the middle of paradise.

"You assumed I was waiting to cheat on you. Is that how you think of me, Danai?" Makhosini sat on the moist grass.

"No, Makho," Danai protested. A vision of Daniel flickered through her mind. "I think sometimes two people meet, fall in love, and promise to be together forever. But life doesn't always go the way we plan." Her voice trailed off.

Makhosini nodded his head and moved closer. "I'm sorry I didn't tell you about Anashe," he whispered. "But I'm furious that you messed around with my boy, and I don't know what to do." Amidst the raging wind and howling trees, Makhosini heard it first—the sound of Danai's brokenness penetrating his soul. He moved closer and erased the gap between them.

They sat together, watching the flowing silhouette of a rich Zimbabwean landscape. Resilient trees blossomed, and sweet scents of African apple trees saturated the air. In the womb of winter, A Peace of Heaven continued to flourish.

"Makho, why have you never tried?"

"Tried what?" he asked.

"Why have you never tried to have sex with me?"

Makhosini's body tightened. "Did you and Derek have sex?" he demanded.

"No! We didn't. I just wondered if you never tried to have sex with me because you are having sex with someone else," Danai blurted. An image of Vanessa floated through her mind.

"Danai, I'm not having sex with you or anyone else because I'm not ready."

"But you must have been ready before. I mean, you have Anashe."

"Exactly! I have Sugarbaby," he replied in a soft yet serious tone. "When Nicki got pregnant, we were both barely fifteen."

"How long did you guys date?"

"We weren't even dating. We were just playing around, and suddenly Nicki was pregnant. We were both too scared to imagine what this would mean to our lives." He stopped talking and pulled Danai onto his lap. "The day after Sugar was born, Nicki's parents came to our house and left Sugar at our door. They left the country with Nicki the following day. Sugar and I never heard from them again. Overnight, I suddenly became a single father but even then, I didn't understand what this baby's existence meant to my life."

"Were you afraid?" She felt him shift uncomfortably.

"I was terrified!" Makhosini chuckled. "When Sugar was six months old, she got sick and couldn't breathe. I took her to Avenues Hospital. The doctor there told me Sugar had bronchiolitis and needed to be admitted to an intensive care unit."

Danai could taste the sadness in Makhosini's voice.

"I didn't have any money, and my parents were in Singapore," Makhosini smiled wryly. "I tried calling my father, but all he could do was wire me the money. It would have taken four days for the money to arrive, and my baby couldn't breathe right then." He stopped speaking and stared into the distance before wrapping her closer in his arms.

"So, what did you do?" Danai asked.

"One of my uncles drove two hours from Gweru just so we could pay for Sugar to be hospitalized. That was the first time I began to

172

understand the weight of my actions and the responsibility that came with being a father."

Danai, Layla, and Thulani often joked about the idea of sex. Their conversations were filled with outrageous humor. In reality, Danai wanted to wait until she was married before sharing that precious part of herself. Listening to Makhosini strengthened her resolve.

"Makho."

"Yes."

"I'm not ready either."

"I know, Danai," he replied. Danai could feel him smiling in the dark.

The sun burst through a purple-glazed sky and caressed everything in sight. In the distance, a radiant Mrs. Volhaagan stuck her head out of the kitchen door. She motioned for Makhosini and Danai to come for breakfast. As they neared the yellow farmhouse, Makhosini looked over at the girl who held his heart in her palm.

"Danai, don't ever cheat on me again," he said and held her tighter.

Chapter Twenty-Six
City of Diamonds

"Aah, Mai Danai! It's a good thing that we bought into that timeshare near Pamuzinda Safari Lodge." Mr. Matamba smiled smugly and dug into his steak. "Christmas season has begun, and this city's already flooded with people who've been living abroad. They are coming back in droves to sample the *new* Harare they've been hearing about."

In the summer of 1991, Harare solidified her reputation as "The City That Rocks." In the blink of an eye, deteriorating buildings transformed into thriving restaurants, elegant boutiques, bars, and exotic beauty spas. Hungry for the coming wave of opportunity, a local millionaire built an entire water park. The rich took the cue and leased their summer houses for exorbitant prices. The poor frantically followed suit, offering services as personal city guides or temporary housekeepers.

"You're right. Sisi Chipo says her travel agency has been completely overwhelmed scheduling trips to Lake Kariba and Victoria Falls." Mrs. Matamba laughed and chopped Mile's steak into tiny pieces. "It's crazy how these returning residents are flooding back from everywhere!"

Armed with bursting suitcases, Gucci handbags, and Oxford shoes, Zimbabwe's returning residents swarmed into Harare International Airport. Residents who'd been living or studying abroad came back to sample a few weeks of the new Harare. Hungry for a taste of the Sunshine City, the mass exodus flew in from Greece, Johannesburg, Lusaka, Sydney, and Lagos. In droves they escaped New York City and Amsterdam's brutal winters. These party troops descended overnight onto the Sunshine City. To the delight of Zimbabwe's Ministry of Tourism, the returning residents dragged along a friend or two from the countries they flew in from.

In anticipation of the Sunshine City's new fame, Sarchies' management team refurbished their club. Overnight, the one-story underground transformed into a three-story dance house with gigantic TV screens built into colorful walls. Weathered sofas were replaced by zebra-print couches and cream-marble tiles. To complete the club's transformation, Sarchies' management team abandoned their legendary members-only policy. The ambitious team built the world's longest bar and opened Sarchies' oak doors to a whole new crowd.

Despite Makhosini and Derek's new jobs, Nyika's intense studying schedule, and Godfrey and Will travelling in and out of the country, the Richlorne crew resumed their role as the kings of Harare's party scene. Decked in trendsetting outfits and expensive shoes, the boys were truly a sight to behold. As returning residents flooded the city, unfamiliar faces thronged into Sarchies' VIP area to meet the ever-popular Richlorne crew. Each new arrival carried his or her own unique story about the joys and hardships of living abroad. Some loudly advertised the excellence of their prestigious university experience. Others boasted about their high-paying jobs and glamorous lifestyles. Unfortunately, too many returnees told tales of discrimination, destitution, oppressive loneliness, and nonstop work hours at minimum wage.

"Oh good, you're here." Makhosini kissed Danai. His eyes appreciatively swept over her form.

She smiled and waved at the rest of the crew. The boys stood in a corner absorbed in a discussion on the upcoming Brazil versus Spain soccer game and an Argentinean player named Diego Maradona. Vanessa sat at one end of the couch next to Nyika. He stood up and joined the soccer conversation. Danai frowned then sat on the couch near Vanessa. Polished with perfectly manicured nails and a glistening cropped afro, Vanessa wore a short red Armani dress that Giorgio must have created specifically for her. Propped next to her gold stilettos lay a classic black-and-white Chanel bag. The girl looked immaculate. Despite the smoky environment, Danai could smell the clear scent of Estée Lauder's Beautiful.

Noting Danai's curiosity, Vanessa uncrossed her legs and moved closer to the girl. Vanessa casually tugged at the straps of her gold stilettos and confidently announced, "I like nice things, so I would never date a guy who couldn't pay my rent or for my lifestyle."

Shocked by the unexpected comment, Danai's eyes darted to Makhosini and the rest of the Richlorne boys. The guys were shamelessly making two-dollar bets over the Spain versus Brazil game. Vanessa must have guessed Danai thoughts because she smiled.

"Exactly!" Vanessa exclaimed.

Amused, Danai laughed with a new understanding. Without hesitation, she moved closer to the girl in the golden stilettos and tried to think of conversation topics.

"Okay, my favorite book of all time is Chinua Achebe's *Things Fall Apart*." Danai giggled, astounded that her and Vanessa shared a passion for classic art and African literature.

"I cried when I read that book and things really fell apart," Vanessa confessed. Her attention turned to a scrawny boy hovering over them. The boy wore a skinny black tie and an oversized red suit. With overflowing confidence, he interrupted the girls' conversation and begged Vanessa for her number.

"Nope." She shook her head.

"Why?" the undeterred boy demanded.

"Why start the engine when the car's going nowhere?" she said, and the girls burst into laughter. Confused, the boy muttered something angrily and left.

"You know, Danai, Makhosini's always been like a brother to me," Vanessa said in a sisterly voice. "We're just friends, and that's all we've ever been."

"I know," Danai shyly answered.

"Makhosini's a good guy, Danai. Treat him good, and he'll love you right. Hold on to what you two have." Vanessa suddenly looked sad and distant. Her eyes flickered toward the boys. To Danai's surprise, Vanessa's gaze rested on Nyika Tumai before she looked away.

The scrawny boy in the red suit reappeared. Reaching past Vanessa, he held out his hand to Danai. Vanessa laughed, and the girls clasped hands. As they held hands, Danai was startled by the roughness of Vanessa's palms. The calloused fingers subtly exposed hardship and poverty. Embarrassed, Vanessa released Danai's hand. She rose and went to join her gentleman friend.

"Are you okay?" Makhosini flopped onto the couch next to his girlfriend.

"Yes, I am."

"Vanessa's something else, right?" Makhosini chuckled and shook his head. "You know, she and Nyika used to be a couple."

"What! Really?" Danai couldn't imagine Nyika paying for Vanessa's lifestyle, let alone making monthly rent payments.

"Yeah, really. She was Nyika's first girlfriend. They met when they were thirteen years old and immediately fell in love. For years they were inseparable. Nyika refused to go anywhere without Vanessa, and that's how she became part of our crew. She was his world, and he was her universe. Back then, Nyika would literally climb walls for her."

"So, what happened?"

"I guess she wouldn't give him what he wanted, and he couldn't give her what she needed."

"What do you mean?"

He looked at Nyika who now stood amid a group of infatuated girls. The girls appeared entranced by his presence. "Nyika craved this

178

world." Makhosini glanced in the opposite direction. "And she thought she needed that world."

Danai watched Vanessa seductively move closer to her latest sugar daddy.

Makhosini rose up from the couch and pulled his woman toward the dance floor.

"Dance with me, Danai," he beckoned. Sade's sultry voice drenched the club and possessed the moment. "Your love is king," the Nigerian singer crooned. Danai looked at her man. He was beautiful. She moved closer and encircled her arms around his neck. "Your love is king," Sade moaned, the strength of her voice ripping through the atmosphere.

Danai glanced over Makhosini's shoulder. Vanessa had returned to their table. With the expression of a little girl who had lost something, she searched the table and looked under the couch. Her hand desperately reached under the couch. A wave of relief swept over her face as she held up a tiny gold chain. The chain glittered brilliantly before it disappeared into the confines of her palm. Only then did Vanessa look up. Her eyes searched the room and stopped when she located Danai. Vanessa smiled and pointed toward the door to gesture that she and her gentleman friend were leaving. Danai waved back. Vanessa followed her companion past the colorful TV screens and zebra couches and out of the oak doors.

"Come with me, Danai," Makhosini beckoned. He grabbed her hand in his.

"Where are we going?" She followed him past the bouncers and out of the building. They crossed the busy road and strolled through

179

Harare City Park. Makhosini slowed down outside Meikles Grand Hotel.

"Yes. You'll do!" he grinned sheepishly. His eyes wandered over Danai's short pink-and-white polka dot dress and thick platform shoes.

"What?" she laughed in amusement.

"Masikati. Welcome to Meikles Grand Hotel," a door attendant said, opening the brass-lined glass doors. The man wore a black tuxedo, white gloves, and a high top hat. Glancing at his silver-cased pocket watch, he said, "Please follow me."

"Welcome to our timeless tradition. High Tea in the Jacaranda Room: 3 p.m. to 5 p.m.," declared an eloquent sign at the entrance. Sweet sounds of classic Bach filled the lounge. Interspersed throughout the room, large potted purple jacaranda trees grew proudly until their branches touched the high ceiling. A lone man relaxed on a corner couch while reading the *Financial Gazette*. Two elderly ladies sipped sherry at a nearby table. One lady read a novel, and the other knitted a sweater.

"Do you like?" Makhosini asked. He settled into a chair opposite Danai.

"How did you find this place?" she exclaimed, glancing around the room in amazement. A waitress appeared and laid out a delicate porcelain tea set, bite size scones, marmalade and clotted cream, tiny raspberry pastries, and an assortment of triangular sandwiches. [1]

"When I was young, I came here once with my mother." Makhosini smiled. "I remember that day like it was yesterday. She woke up singing. She was like a little girl who had discovered a new secret. We came here and sat right there." He pointed at a table in the

180

center of the lounge. "'Makho,' my mother confided in me, 'Today is April eighteenth, 1980. It's Zimbabwe's first Independence Day. We're finally free, Makho, and today your father told me he loves me.'"

Danai smiled as she imagined a younger Mrs. Moyo sitting amidst the blossoming purple Jacaranda trees, excitedly celebrating her love and the independence of her country.

Makhosini picked up a small scone topped with raspberry jam and whipped cream and lifted it to Danai's mouth. She tasted the sweet delicacy and sighed loudly. Amused by her reaction, Makhosini laughed and kissed falling crumbs from the corner of her mouth.

He wiped the sweat off his eyebrow and stared at the laughing girl. He reached into his jacket and pulled out a small box neatly wrapped in gold gift wrapping. Makhosini carefully pulled out an exquisite diamond pendant hanging on a delicate rose-gold chain and placed it around his girlfriend's neck.

"Before I knew you, I loved you, Danai," he whispered and kissed the arch of her neck. "I will always love you, Danai Matamba."

Chapter Twenty-Seven
The Honey That Weeps

"You're what?" Godfrey's eyes darted between Makhosini and their lanky friend who was standing at the end of the bar. Nyika stood alone. Remorse masked Nyika's expression, and his gaze remained glued on his shoes. Ignoring Nyika, Godfrey grimaced at their surroundings. They'd come to a sleazy joint in the middle of nowhere. Determined to celebrate the birth of 1992, their group arrived early. By midnight, the joint's parking lot remained desolate and empty. Just when Godfrey believed their night couldn't get worse, Makhosini made his shocking announcement. Stupefied, Godfrey's glare rested on his friend before scowling at an elderly DJ blasting hits from the 1960s.

"I'm leaving," Makhosini repeated.

"Why? When?" Godfrey eyes instinctively darted back to Nyika.

"In two weeks—"

"What do you mean, you're leaving?" Danai interrupted with rising panic.

"I got accepted into the University of Sydney." Makhosini reached past Lillian and Layla and pulled his girlfriend closer. "I didn't say anything because I was waiting for the university to approve my financial aid. Yesterday they called to let me know I've been approved." His gaze moved from Danai to his best friend, still standing in the distance. Drenched in despair, Nyika turned away and staggered out of the dilapidated building.

"But I thought we agreed that you would wait until I finished high school and then we'd go to varsity together," Danai blurted.

"I know. We did. But this year has been so frustrating." Contempt coated Makhosini's voice. "It feels like everyone's doing their own thing, and I'm here floating in a job that I can't stand. I'm being overworked like a dog and treated worse than one."

"Couldn't you just look for another job until we leave together?" Her heated gaze desperately wandered from Makhosini to their friends.

"Babe, I'm tired." His fingers nervously trailed through his hair. "You can't imagine how it feels to watch the days of your life slip away while everyone else's dreams seem to be unfolding."

"But what about me?" Danai moaned, ignoring Lillian's leave-it-alone expression.

"What about *me*, Danai? It's not always about you!" Makhosini retorted.

"You said we'd stay together. That you would never leave me." Danai struggled to breathe. She'd seen the faraway look in Makhosini eyes as the returning residents recounted stories of their lives abroad. He'd listened intently while the returnees arrogantly described their university lives and boasted about their high-paying jobs. He'd openly expressed sympathy for those who'd endured discrimination and oppressive loneliness while living in foreign lands, but how had Danai missed Makhosini's discontentment? The type of frustration that made a man simply want to pack up and leave, regardless of what lay ahead. Ironically, Makhosini looked peaceful for the first time in months.

"I have to go, babe." Makhosini reached past Lillian to hug his girlfriend. "We'll only be apart for a year until you finish high school. You'll come, and we'll be together again."

Danai pulled away. Her gaze absorbed the dingy club. The club appeared emptier now than when they'd first arrived.

"You promised we'd stay together," she whimpered. Her agony pouring forth from within. With tears clouding her vision, Danai rose from her seat and stumbled toward the exit.

Chapter Twenty-Eight
Love Don't Live Here

"Why did I come here?" Danai breathed. She ignored her discarded shoe and treaded through the muddy landscape, deeper into the womb of greenery. Her eyes flickered up towards the forceful summer sun. Perfectly molded hills decorated with swaying ancient trees stood in the distance. A sharp breeze swept through her dress, prompting Danai to wrap her sweater tightly around her body. She glanced back at the taxi driver patiently waiting in his van.

"I shouldn't have come here," she muttered, moving out of the sun's path into the shadows. Towering trees cleared and gave rise to a clear view of the lake. Brilliant sun rays pierced the water's surface, creating an illusion of millions of floating diamonds. Squatting at the edge of the water, she dipped her fingers into the cool water and washed her face. She sat at the water's edge and watched fluttering birds and a lone blue butterfly.

"My world is changing, yet this place remains the same," Danai whispered, staring at A Peace of Heaven. "Everyone keeps telling me I'm supposed to be celebrating. But how can I be happy when a part of me is leaving?"

"Who says you should be happy?" A voice interrupted her solitude.

Startled, Danai turned and stared at the figure approaching her. "What are you doing here, Makhosini?" She noted the dark circles under his eyes. Sadness masked Makhosini's expression as he held her discarded shoe.

"Everyone is telling me that I should be happy," he said, moving closer to her. His eyes surveyed the peaceful landscape. "But how can I celebrate when I'm leaving a part of me?"

The sweet scents of African apple trees saturated his nostrils. He crouched down and settled at the edge of the waterbed next to his woman.

"Everything is changing, but will we remain the same?" The wind bitterly cut into Makhosini's words. His gaze remained on the lake, yet his eyes were filled with uncertainty. Shattering intangible barriers, the distinctive melody of an African nightingale filled the atmosphere. Soft yet powerful, the nightingale's song rippled through the landscape. Surprised, Danai's gaze moved to the crooning bird before flickering back to Makhosini. He seemed to have grown thinner in the week since she last saw him.

"Are you okay?" she asked.

Makhosini shook his head and stared at the ground beneath him.

"I knew you were trouble that night you first kissed me two years ago." She smiled as tears flowed down her cheeks.

"I knew I loved you before I met you." He grinned sadly. He glanced at a flutter of blue butterflies dancing around the couple. With fingers intertwined, Makhosini and Danai sat on the muddy waterbed and watched the sky transform herself from purple to a fiery yellow.

"There's somewhere I want to take you. Will you come with me?" Danai scooted to her feet.

He slowly nodded and rose from the water bank.

They stepped out of the taxi onto an overcrowded street lined with several Zimco buses. Women balancing suitcases on their heads rushed past the couple, causing Makhosini to instinctively grab Danai's hand.

"Come and get them now. They'll be gone tomorrow." A shrewd vendor advertised his selection of the latest CD players.

Makhosini frowned at Mbare Musika's aging infrastructure. The place was in desperate need of repair. Avoiding swarms of insatiable vendors and hungry street kids, Danai and Makhosini weaved between rows of carrots, dried kale, and crates of sweet potatoes. The aroma of mature bananas and ripened mangos tickled Makhosini senses, reminding him that he hadn't eaten in days.

"Good afternoon, Sekuru," Danai called to an elderly man, then turned to greet the man's wife who stood at a stall entrance. The man sat on the ground while restoring discarded furniture. "That sekuru takes the stuff people throw away and makes something new." Danai explained and led Makhosini to the man's trading post. Makhosini stepped into the stall and gasped, surprised at the assembly of newly refurbished furniture. Each piece of furniture had been redesigned to produce a perfect replica of famous mid-century styles. In one corner, a collection of Louis XVI style armchairs encircled a mahogany Chippendale cabinet.

"One day, when you come back, I want you to buy me one of those." Danai pointed to a set of emerald-green and gold upholstered accent chairs.

"When I return, I will give you anything you want." Makhosini chuckled and held her hand.

"Follow me," she said, giggling.

Mai Chenai stirred okra stew with a swift movement. Her piercing gaze moved from the pot to a couple entering Alice's Shabeen.

"Aah, what is this, Danai? You've finally come back." Mai Chenai wiped the sweat from her forehead and descended from her small ledge. She watched the couple wading through the thicket of customers until they stood next to her. Her eyes slowly assessed Makhosini. "And you—where have you been?" She sucked in her breath and shook her head.

Surprised, Danai's gaze darted from the shabeen owner to Makhosini, who was grinning sheepishly next to her.

"They've been coming here since they were little boys." Mai Chenai giggled at Danai's confusion. She grabbed their hands and led them farther into the compound.

"When we were young, Derek, Will B., Nyika, and I would ride our BMX bikes to Mbare Musika," Makhosini explained. "The other guys stopped coming when we grew up."

"But he and Nyika keep coming here and bothering me year after year." Mai Chenai rolled her eyes in feigned annoyance.

"Nyika loves Mai Chenai's cooking." Makhosini grinned.

The hut's rusty metal door swung open, and Mai Chanai's eldest son, Cautious, strolled out of the hut. "We heard you're moving to Aussie," he bellowed.

"Is it true?" Mai Chenai asked, and Makhosini nodded. "Aah, our baby is leaving us," she moaned. A lone tear trickled down her face.

"Nyika came here last week. He told everyone you were leaving," Cautious shouted. He pointed to a lone crate near the hut's entrance. "Nyika sat over there, crying like a baby while he guzzled down the sadza. Aah, a man shouldn't cry like that!" Cautious chuckled and shook his head.

"Maybe if you showed a little sensitivity and cried like that, then these customers would buy some of your art!" Mai Chenai barked. She dramatically waved her finger to the paintings hanging on the barbed wire fence. Danai burst into giggles and watched Makhosini laugh.

"Come, Makhosini," Danai reached for her boyfriend's hand and led him toward two crates in the center of Alice's Shabeen. "Let's eat."

Chapter Twenty-Nine
The Wind that Blows Away

O n a rainy afternoon in January 1992, Mr. Matamba, Miles, and Danai trudged into Harare International Airport. Makhosini stood next to his parents in the departure area. In a nearby seating area, his four sisters sat with Sugarbaby and Richard, Makhosini's brother-in-law. Shortly after the Matambas' arrival, Derek, Nyika, and Will B. rushed in with Lilly and Godfrey trailing behind them. Within minutes, several of Makhosini's relatives clamored into the Harare airport. The adults excitedly greeted each other and gathered into small groups. Older kids went on errands to buy snacks, while the younger children freely ran throughout the airport.

"Who's going, Daddy?" Sugarbaby approached her father.

"I'm going, Anashe." Makhosini replied for the tenth time that day. Lifting his daughter into his arms, he held her tightly. "I'm going, baby."

"Okay, Daddy," the five-year-old shouted, and Makhosini set her back on her feet. "I'm going to Australia, too!" Sugar confidently announced.

No one heard Makhosini's response, but a loud scream ripped through Harare International airport.

"No, Daddy," Sugar screeched. "You not leaving me. I want to go with you."

Danai's lips dried up. Her tongue stuck to the roof of her mouth. Salty tears gushed down her face. Within seconds, Miles began wailing too. Shocked, Sugarbaby stopped crying and stared at Miles and Danai.

"Who are these people?" Makhosini's uncle demanded. His heated gaze oscillated between the siblings.

"Did we pay bride price for her?" Makhosini's grandmother inquired.

"No, but you never know these days, aah," his aunt bellowed.

"Maybe she's pregnant, and he's running away to America," one man concluded.

"Danai is not pregnant, and Makhosini isn't going to America. He's going to the University of Sydney in Australia," Makhosini's cousin corrected her father. She gave Danai a sympathetic smile, and Miles and Danai wept louder.

"Who's even heard of the University of Sydney?" Miles demanded between sobs. "Why couldn't he just stay here and go to the University of Zimbabwe?" He resumed crying with greater intensity.

Embarrassed, Mr. Matamba grabbed his children and briskly ushered them toward a stairwell leading to the viewing terrace.

"You know, these kids, they are losing their best friend," Mr. Matamba apologetically explained to the glowering adults.

As the Matambas ascended the staircase, Makhosini suddenly appeared next to Baba. "Take care of your sister for me." He grinned and gave Miles a brotherly hug. "And remember to hang up on any guy who calls the house asking for her."

Miles obediently nodded and wiped away his remaining tears.

"Are you okay?" Makhosini held onto Danai's hand. Despite Miles and Baba's presence and his family watching in the distance, he leaned over and intimately kissed his girlfriend.

"I miss you already, Little Girl. Promise I'll call you as soon as I arrive." She heard him whisper, and that's when Danai felt Makhosini's tears rolling down her face.

An hour later, Air Zimbabwe proudly made its course down the long runway. Danai stood on the crowded terrace and watched the Boeing 767 gracefully glide into the night then disappear into a dark velvety sky. Without a word, she stared at the star-drenched sky, yearning for something that had already left.

Chapter Thirty
Redemption Songs

"Happy birthday, Miles!" Mrs. Matamba clung tightly to her son. "I can't believe my baby is thirteen years old."

"I'm a man now," Miles shouted, pulling away. Ignoring the tears streaming down his mother's face, he stepped out of the Matamba house to enter his first year of high school at Falcon High Boarding School.

"It's funny how he's beginning at our end," Thulani poetically described the girls' final year of high school.

"What's crazy is that Miles agreed to go so far away," Danai chuckled. "He's literally moving a whole day's journey away and didn't even cry about it."

The year 1992 ushered in profound changes for the Matamba family. Riding on the success of his city office, Mr. Matamba launched a second law office in Chitungwiza. With Baba preoccupied with his new clientele and Miles in boarding school, Mrs. Matamba decided to embark on her dream. She hired two assistants and purchased a small van. With a little effort, Danai's mother transformed their kitchen into a viable catering business.

In a different suburb, Mrs. Patel chased Dr. S. D. Patel out of his home office. She unlocked three adjoining rooms and launched her Saturday Super SAT Prep program. To Baba's amusement, Layla and Danai voluntarily signed up and joined eight other students in Mrs. Patel's prep class.

At Mrs. Matamba's insistence, the girls enrolled in driving classes. Danai earned her driver's license after the fourth attempt.

"Now you can help me pick up groceries on weekends and drive Mbuya to her doctor visits." Mrs. Matamba chuckled.

"Nyika!" Danai left Mrs. Patel's class one afternoon and was strolling through the city when she saw him in the distance. Dressed in a conservative gray suit, Nyika Tumai clung to a beige briefcase. He frantically avoided the angry traffic and hastily made his way across a double-lane street.

"Nyika, hey," Danai shouted. She hadn't seen him in the months following Makhosini's departure. Surprised, he stopped and looked in her direction. He smiled and walked through the shouting street vendors.

"Little Girl, it's been too long. How are you?" Nyika asked.

"Hi Nyika. It's been a long time." Danai laughed. "How are you? Where have you been?"

Lifting his beige briefcase, Nyika announced, "I've joined the world of grown-ups, Little Girl. I'm working at Price Water House during the day and studying for my finance exams at night." He grinned at the look of surprise on Danai's face.

"Life is work—home then work again for me!" Nyika declared, pulling out a crinkled business card.

For the first time, Danai noticed the dark areas encircling his eyes. Dry coffee stains tainted his sky-blue tie, and the wrinkled shirt did little to improve his appearance. Nyika looked tired and unkempt.

Ignoring her worried expression, Nyika grinned and asked, "Hey, when was the last time you talked to Makhosini? How is Aussie treating my boy?"

They stood on the sidewalk, silently observing rushing pedestrians and the desperate traffic. "He's fine." Danai smiled. "So, are you guys going to Eddy's barbecue-braai next Saturday?"

"Can't, Little Girl. I think I'm working that weekend. And you?"

"No, I don't think I can," she said, and that was the moment Danai knew their world had changed.

Nyika glanced at his watch and mumbled a quick goodbye before he headed back to Price Water House. He left Danai standing alone on the sidewalk.

Despite her increasingly demanding schedule, Danai rejoined Peter Birch School of Art for Saturday evening art classes. She'd grown older and become curious about how far she could carry her talent. A month into their classes, the instructor invited the group to display works for the Night of the Artist Gala at Harare Art Gallery. Danai submitted two pieces. Her first presentation, entitled *My Nest*, depicted Harare.

With the use of charcoal and vivid oil paints, Danai recreated the Sunshine City with all its intricacies: the towering high-rise buildings, screeching minivans, luxury cars, and decadent stores surrounded by hungry street kids and their homeless mothers.

The Night of the Artist Gala turned out to be a huge fundraising event for the city. The black-tie event attracted people from all walks of life—art lovers, philanthropists, diplomats, business owners and company representatives. Harare's mayor arrived shortly after the opening ceremony. The youthful mayor welcomed guests during an informal cocktail hour. He gave a short speech on the importance of the city's cultural development. The mayor shook hands with two visiting ambassadors before excusing himself and leaving to attend another ceremony.

"Is that my girl?" a voice playfully asked. Surprised, Danai turned and found Thulani standing behind her. Thulani had dressed up for the event. She stood with her boyfriend, Giles, smiling and holding his hand.

"I can't believe you guys actually came!" Danai joyfully hugged her friend.

"What? Danai, did you really think we'd miss this?" Thulani's eyes shone in admiration. "I mean, you've finally moved up from Alice's Shabeen to the big leagues. Yes, someone definitely had to witness this."

An hour after Giles and Thulani's impromptu appearance, Mr. and Mrs. Matamba walked in with Miles trailing behind them.

"Wow, Mama, you look glamorous!" Danai gasped.

Ignoring her husband's annoyed expression, Mrs. Matamba gracefully twirled to show off her long black satin dress.

"She took too long getting dressed, and that's why we're late." Mr. Matamba grumbled, tugging at his bow tie. To Danai's amusement, her mother rolled her eyes and twirled a second time. The Matambas joined Thulani, Danai, and Giles and strode through the gallery browsing several displayed works of forty artists.

At the Night of The Artist finale, each artist received a check and watched their creative works carried away to the holding room. A representative for Schweppes Bottling Company procured *My Nest*, while "Mr. and Mrs. Matamba of Roseberry Lane" won the bid for Danai's second piece titled *My Self Portrait*.

"Danai?" His smile drew her attention before she heard his voice. It had been two weeks since the Night of the Artist Gala. With her check in hand, Danai had driven into the city to open her first saving account. She walked into the tiny blue coffee shop on the quiet end of Karigamombe Center and heard him. "Danai," the raspy voice crooned.

"Daniel?" Her eyes widened in surprise.

"How are you?" Daniel laughed. His voice still held a familiar friendliness. He'd grown taller and more muscular. The towering box-cut had been replaced by a close fade, which gave Daniel's face a more chiseled appearance. His once familiar boyish walk had transformed into a confident manly stride.

"How are you, girl?" He pulled out a chair for her and sat in the opposite seat.

197

"Danny, it's really you! I've been good. What are you doing here?" she asked.

"Oh, I'm waiting for my girlfriend. Why are you women always late?" He glanced at his watch and chuckled.

They sat in the crowded blue café drinking iced watermelon tea. In an obscure corner, Daniel and Danai quenched the day's voracious heat, and three years of silence.

"Are you serious?" Danai laughed in disbelief. "You became a schoolteacher! I thought you hated high school."

"Teaching's actually very rewarding work." Daniel grinned. He taught Geography and World History to children in a remote village. "For me, this is more than just a job. The work I do is my purpose."

"Really." Danai eyes slowly assessed the man sitting before her.

"Most of my students' families can barely afford books, so the funding we get from non-profit organizations is heaven sent," he explained. "Once a month I commute from the village back to the city and see my family and friends."

"I'm both impressed and surprised." Danai smiled.

"And you? You look happy. Did something happen?"

"Oh, I just opened my first savings account and deposited my first check." She waved her bank statement at him.

"Well, congratulations. I hope that money was well earned." He smiled. "I see you're growing up, Miss Danai Matamba."

"You know, I bumped into your father last year. It was kind of weird. I didn't know what to say to him," Danai confessed. "Our relationship ended so suddenly. When we parted ways, we never got to say goodbye."

"You and my dad?" Daniel grinned mischievously.

"You and me, Daniel." Danai rolled her eyes at his humor.

"I know. But seriously, do you know that my dad still asks about you? I think he's still mourning our breakup," he chuckled. With a glimmer of regret in his eyes, Daniel looked through window and watched the increasing crowd. Harare was growing.

"Back then it was just too hard to say goodbye, Danai." Through the small window, Daniel watched street vendors frantically competing for customers. "Do you still love him?" he asked.

"Your dad?" Danai asked.

"No, Makhosini. I heard he left."

"Yes, he did. It's been almost a year." She smiled and took a sip of the watermelon tea, "And yes, I think I'll always love him. Does that sound pathetic after what happened with us?"

"No, it doesn't sound pathetic." Daniel tasted his strawberry swirl ice cream. "I saw you with Makhosini at Nyika's birthday party three years ago. You guys were arguing on the stairwell, but I remember looking at your face and thinking, *she looks really happy*. At first, I felt angry, but everything fell into place, and seeing you two together made moving on easier."

"And you, Danny? What happened to the girl you met at a party?" she asked.

"Oh, that ended after only a month." Daniel shook his head and laughed. "Danai." He stared at her.

"Yes, Daniel."

"I know you didn't cheat on me." He glanced at her apple pie. "Back then, I heard bits and pieces of what really happened, but I was seventeen. For a seventeen-year-old boy, rep is everything. At that time, other people's opinion was more important than us."

"The rep?" Danai grinned and knowingly shook her head.

"Yes, that reputation!" Daniel placed his hand over his eyes and laughed. He uncovered his eyes and watched a young couple rushing across the street while avoiding the unruly traffic.

"You are good man, Danny." Danai smiled thoughtfully. "You always were. Back then I was too young to understand how precious you were and the value of what we had."

"We were really something else back then." He laughed softly at the memory of him and Danai running passionately through a field of mango trees.

"Yes, we were something else," Danai agreed. She pointed at a speaker in the corner of the café and giggled in surprise. "Oooh, I haven't heard that song in years," she exclaimed.

"Oh that's Ten City, and the song is called 'That's The Way Love Is,'" Daniel stated. "It's a song about me and you." He grinned sheepishly, and Danai burst into laughter. Like two old friends meeting at the crossroads of life, they sat unified in that moment.

"Danny, I have to go. I need to stop by the QVC pharmacy before picking up Mbuya from her doctor's appointment." Danai rose from her seat, "I'm glad we met today. It was good seeing you again."

"Yes, it was good seeing you too." Daniel smiled and slowly rose from his seat. "Goodbye, Danai Matamba."

"Goodbye, Daniel Munya Tashaya."

Clutching her grandmother's medications, Danai stepped out of QVC pharmacy and glanced across the street. Amidst the rushing pedestrians and screaming vendors, a couple quietly strolled outside Karigamombe Business Center. Step by step, the couple moved in unison. Daniel Tashaya's girlfriend's outfit matched her boyfriend's. She wore baggy green jeans and a bright orange sweater. The short girl clutched Daniel's hand and proudly walked next to him. The man at the girl's side sharply contrasted that boy who'd worn a T-shirt declaring, "Layla, Danai, Sibo, Daniel, and Thulani, Harare Show 1989."

Oblivious to anyone watching them, Daniel and his companion walked toward Madombo Jewelry. They glared at an extravagant display of Zimbabwean diamond engagement rings. His girlfriend enthusiastically pointed at the glimmering rings, and Daniel nodded.

"That man once was my boyfriend," Danai whispered to herself. A long time ago, Daniel had desperately burst into her life and settled in her heart. They clung onto each other's hands while dancing in the singing rain and running between blossoming mango trees.

"He was my first love." She smiled thoughtfully. As Danai drove further away, she glanced into her rearview mirror. In the distance, Daniel opened Madombo Jewelry's glass door. He followed his girlfriend into the store, and in the flicker of a moment, Daniel Munya Tashaya vanished back into the whispers of the past.

Chapter Thirty-One
Willow Meade Manor

"Hey, do you guys believe that there's only two months left, and then it's goodbye high school forever?" Thulani sighed.

"I'm kind of scared," Nina confessed. After her ex-roommate Sibo was expelled from the school—along with Sharice and the Tattlers—for inciting general discontentment, Nina had moved into Thulani's room. The two became fast friends. It had only been two months, but Nina had become comfortable enough with all three girls to share her innermost fears.

"I mean, it's like we're grown-ups now and we can do anything, but I feel like I don't know a thing about being an adult. I don't know if there are any opportunities for someone like me," she mumbled. Despite her scholarship, Nina's parents worked day and night to afford their daughter attending the prestigious boarding school. While her friends prepared their university applications, Nina could barely afford bus fare.

Boisterous sounds of the Marimba band drenched the night air and interrupted their conversation. Candlelit tables surrounded by appreciative patrons enhanced Willow Meade's scenic garden setting.

"Guys, we are at Willow Meade Manor! It's my *birthday,* and you guys are really sucking the joy out of it," Layla blurted. She frowned at a young boy rushing past their table.

"Oh right, happy birthday, Layla!" the girls chanted. Seated beneath a rich starry sky and surrounded by blossoming peach trees, Thulani, Nina, and Danai celebrated Layla's eighteenth birthday. Thulani invited Giles, while Miles tagged along as the girls' special guest.

"What's up, Layla? You look so down." Danai leaned over and held her friend's hand.

"Last night my father sat me down," Layla said, disappointment marring her expression. "He's refusing to cosign my university applications. Says he's not paying for me to go to varsity."

"What?" Thulani and Danai yelled.

"Yes! He told me that I had two simple options. Option number one is I work as an errand girl at one of his clinics. The second option is that I find a husband and get married immediately!"

"Are you joking?" Danai choked on her guava juice. "Is he serious?"

"Very serious. He said that either way, I must leave his house the day we finish high school. He claims my stepmother isn't comfortable about having another grown woman living in *her* house." Layla rolled her eyes.

"Wow, it must have taken him all of ten minutes to come up with that one," Thulani remarked angrily. "All that money and no sense! I can't believe your father's thinking."

"Well, why don't you just apply for financial aid?" Nina asked.

"She doesn't qualify," Danai answered. "Her father's too rich!"

"Also, in order to be approved for an international student visa, she has to show documents proving that Dr. Njeke is going to financially support her during her four years of university," Thulani added.

"I'm really annoyed," Layla sighed. "After all these years my stepmother is still trying to manipulate my life when she should be pruning her own garden."

A disgruntled waiter appeared and took their order.

"Wait! What do you mean?" Giles asked.

"Well," Thulani began, "Last year Layla's father went to Gweru and paid bride price for an unknown young lady. Unbeknownst to Layla's stepmother, Dr. Njeke has secretly taken on a second wife and opened his own small house. His new wife is only twenty-five years old!"

"What?" Giles stared at all three girls.

"According to Layla's aunt, this new wife is demanding to move out of the small house and into the main house. She wants to move up, you see!" Danai shook her head.

"She's young and ambitious, and she's not playing games," Thulani blurted. "That girl has spent the past year ruthlessly petitioning Layla's grandmother and aunts to plead her cause. She showers them with gifts and buys groceries for them."

"But what does Layla's stepmother say?" Giles gulped in shock.

"She doesn't know!" Layla chuckled. "My stepmother doesn't even realize that there's a second wife who's already pruning her garden."

"Wow, that's really crazy," Giles mumbled. A vision of his own parents flickered through his mind. His parents often quibbled about politics and their in-laws, but they loved each other unconditionally. Giles had never seen his father look at another woman.

"Basically, it looks like Layla's stepmother will be moving out before Layla does!" Danai giggled.

"You know what's crazy—when I was a kid and my father was married to my mother, my stepmother did to my mother the exact same thing that woman is doing now," Layla sighed. "That's how my stepmother entered our home. Now she's trying to kick me out and calling it *her* home!"

"Ah, that's too crazy!" Thulani's voice shot through the music.

"Layla, why don't you go live with your real mother?" Nina suggested.

"And listen to her husband rant and rave about not wanting another man's child under his roof? That man despises my very existence." Layla's lip quivered in anger. "They've been struggling financially for as long as I can remember. To him, I'm just an extra mouth to feed."

"You're probably better off choosing one of Dr. Njeke's ridiculous options," Thulani agreed. She motioned for the waiter to return.

"I don't understand. How did you end up living with your dad instead of your mother?" Nina asked.

"She conned him." Danai laughed.

"What? How?" Nina stared at her friends in surprise.

"I was eleven years old when my father kicked my mother and me out. I love my mother, but I knew the only way to survive was school. If I didn't get an education, I would end up like my mother, marrying a man like my father." Layla smiled at her friends' stunned expressions. Thoughts of her father filled her mind. Dr. Njeke was a wealthy and powerful man with many shortcomings. His greatest weakness was his elderly mother. "One night I snuck out of the shack my mother and I were living in. I caught a bus to the village to stay with my father's mother."

"She cried every day until her grandmother dragged her back to Dr. Njeke's house." Danai giggled.

"My grandmother threatened my father. She told him she would never see him again unless he took care of me and sent me to the best school." Layla winked at her friends. "My father's really scared of his mother."

"Weren't you scared?" Nina asked.

"I was terrified, but I had to survive." Layla grinned.

"You're going to have to find a way to survive again," Danai said thoughtfully.

"Three letters for you, Danai," Miles interjected. "UNC!"

Danai scowled at her brother, and her friends burst into laughter.

"But what's gon' happen to us? We'll all have to go our separate ways," Nina mumbled. She glanced over at the girl seated opposite her. Layla was outgoing and often outspoken. Dubbed by the other students as "The Prada Princess," Layla wrapped herself in the latest designer wear and would often spend more money in a day than Nina's parents made in a year. While Nina pushed through crowded bus stops, Layla was chauffeured to and from school. They had always seemed so different, but today, as Nina listened to Layla's story, she felt closer to her than she did the other girls.

"Don't worry, my princess," Miles announced. To Danai's dismay, her brother reached out and stroked Nina's hand. "If you just let me be your man, I'll be right here with you."

"Miles, stop that right now or I'll take you home," Danai scolded her brother.

"I can't wait for high school to end." Thulani chuckled. "I'm ready for something new." She shyly glanced at Giles, who gave her an affectionate look. "Like getting married, my own home and babies, and having my own maid to boss around."

"That just sounds like bills and a lot of responsibility," Danai muttered.

"It's the promise of a new beginning." Thulani burst into laughter. "The next season in our lives, Danai!"

"Aah, this is all too depressing. Let's change the subject." Layla sat up in her chair. "Hey, you know, our Leavers Ball is next month. Am I the only one who still hasn't gotten a gown?"

With the caressing night breeze and dancing candle flames, the earlier ambience returned.

"It's gift and cake time!" Thulani announced. A burst of excitement swept through the air as the Marimba band played a Shona version of Frankie Beverly's "Before I Let You Go." While couples rose from their seats and made their way onto the dance floor, Danai dragged Layla and Miles to the stage where they danced to the band's last song.

On October twenty-fourth, 1992, Lillian and Godfrey exchanged vows before a sea of guests in an elaborate outdoor ceremony. Amidst blossoming trees and colorful flowers, scores of guests seated at linen-covered tables toasted this breathtaking union of two families. Bradley, Godfrey's younger brother, stood in as the best man, and Danai was Lilly's maid of honor. Champagne glasses clinked, and laughter soaked the atmosphere. Godfrey wept as he recited his vows, while a radiant Lillian glowed beautifully. Shouts of joy filled the air as Godfrey intimately kissed his new wife and then cut their seven-tiered wedding cake.

"Little Girl, how are you?" a male voice asked. Surprised, Danai looked up. Derek stood in front of her. He was dressed in an elegant three-piece suit and smiling. Derek introduced Magnolia, his fiancée. Magnolia promptly showed off her exquisite pear-shaped engagement ring.

"How are you, Derek?" Danai shifted uncomfortably. "It's been a long time."

"Yeah, it has been a long time. How are you, Danai?"

"I'm good," she reluctantly answered. Despite Danai's unfriendly tone, Derek and Magnolia excitedly chattered about the amazing ceremony and marveled at how beautiful the bride looked. Eventually the couple left to greet other guests. As they left, Derek abruptly turned and walked back toward Danai.

"I'd hoped I'd see you today. Can we talk?" he asked.

"Yes, okay," she hesitantly replied.

He settled into a seat next to her. "Danai, I should have said this long time ago." Derek nervously ran his fingers over his hair as he

208

spoke. "I'm really sorry for the problems I caused between Makhosini and you."

With Derek's apology, the icy tension between them eased, and Danai's thinly veiled anger began melting away. She winced at the memory of the night they sat on the floor separated by pills and a beer bottle.

"I'm sorry, too, Derek," Danai confessed. "Are you okay now?"

"Yes, I'm doing good." His familiar grin appeared. "I'm working. I manage a small grocery store that my mother set up in Highfields township. So, now I help to take care of my siblings."

"Wow, that's nice, Derek. How is your family doing?" Danai asked.

"We're okay. We joined a support group that meets once a week for people who've lost their parents to AIDS or whose parents are living with HIV."

"How is your mother?"

"She's doing okay. She's still in and out of hospital, but you know how it is these days."

"Yeah, I know." Danai sighed sadly.

"Danai, I really am sorry for everything." He sounded sincere, and she believed him.

"Derek."

"Yes, Danai."

"Thank you for this moment, and thank you for every moment when we were friends." She smiled. "And congratulations on your engagement."

"Thank you, Danai." Derek rose from his seat. "I stopped by your father's law office a couple times, but he wasn't in. I wanted to thank

209

him personally for what he did for me and my family." Noting her confused expression, Derek explained, "Your baba paid for all my mother's and my hospital fees. We only found out a couple of months ago when we tried to settle the hospital bills. Your baba also petitioned the court for a judgment awarding my mother the right to keep our house and ordering my father to financially support his children. Please thank your baba for me." He smiled and gave her a brotherly hug. "It was good seeing you again, Little Girl." Derek walked off to join Magnolia who stood patiently waiting in the distance.

"Hey, Derek was here earlier, and we spoke," Danai confided in Godfrey. "By the way, where's Nyika? Isn't he coming to the wedding?"

"Oh, didn't you hear?" Godfrey asked.

"No, hear what?"

"Price Water House transferred Nyika to Switzerland a month ago. They offered him a nice condo and a sweet paycheck, and of course, Nyika grabbed the offer and jumped on that plane." Godfrey chuckled.

"Really, oh wow! Does he like Switzerland?"

"You know Nyika—new places, new waters! He says he's a little lonely, but he's living lavishly on that finance money." Godfrey laughed and shook his head. Danai smiled as she imagined Nyika dancing to imaginary music and blowing his golden whistle in Europe.

Eighteen years later, Danai would be on a Qantas flight from Brisbane to Nairobi when she would browse through the in-flight magazine. That month's issue focused on the ten most influential men transforming the trend of global economics. Number eight was Mr. Nyika Tumai, CEO and owner of the Swiss-based Revival Bank.

Astounded by a picture of Nyika impeccably dressed in a black tuxedo and casually leaning on his A380 private jet, Danai would turn to the article. Despite steaks of gray gracing his hairline and the occasional age line treading across his cheek, Nyika's photo defied time. According to the in-flight article, Mr. Tumai's Revival Bank was changing the face of global banking by encouraging investment in developing countries. Nyika Tumai confidently declared: "These developing countries financed the progression of the now developed countries. It only makes sense that developed countries should invest in the very countries that helped establish them. In so doing, they open new markets and greater opportunities for their own companies. From a business perspective, developing countries are the cradle of most of the world's raw and untapped wealth. Countries like Zimbabwe house massive, insurmountable stores of gold, platinum, and diamonds. To invest in these countries is simply good business sense. Everyone wins! I mean, it's going to happen with or without you, so you might as well jump on this bandwagon."

As the Zimbabwean sun set and the wedding reception ended, the newlyweds thanked their families and guests. Lilly threw her bouquet, and the couple left for their honeymoon at Mozambique's Macaneta Beach.

A month after Godfrey and Lillian's wedding, the girls wrote their final A-level examinations and, in an instant, high school ended.

"Ladies, you came here as little girls, and today you leave as women." Mr. Ritchie, the school's headmaster, gave his closing speech at their last school assembly. "Your teachers, matrons, and I did all we could, and it's now time to pass the baton onto you."

Thulani wept, and Nina stood in shock. Layla and Danai danced. Leaning over the podium, Mr. Ritchie asserted, "Ladies, the world is yours and your time is now. Fulfill your dreams, achieve great successes, and hopefully in ten or twenty years, you'll come back and tell us all about it."

"You're coming, right?" Danai urged Nina after their final assembly. The girls stood in the school parking lot surrounded by a sea of students and their endless suitcases. "We're going to Ashley and Mudiwa's party tonight."

"Thulani and I are spending the night at Danai's house. We're all wearing gold and purple." Layla's excitement resonated throughout the parking lot. "Girl, you have to come."

"You know, it's our last party in high school and it's gonna be the best party ever!" Thulani exclaimed.

"Party of the decade!" Layla echoed. And it truly was the best party of that decade.

Chapter Thirty-Two
Makhosini's Song

I'm the cool breeze on a hot summer night.

A fountain of water to thirsty land.

Hungry soil for tears of rain,

That ray of hope at the completion of every day.

Bread to your butter, honey seductive laughter

That thought behind your succulent smile.

Yes, I'm that brother.

A cool breeze on a hot summer night.

—"Powers of Petals"

"Makhosini! Where are you? Spring 2012 is here!"

Amid scent-drenched Sakura cherry blossom trees, passionate tourists overflowed into New York City's streets. Another brutal winter had ended, and Brooklyn's neighborhoods reawakened to the bodacious sounds of street jazz and dancing grandmas. Hungry to escape the stifling confines of their winter hideouts, laughing teenagers swarmed into Brooklyn's corner-stores. Lovers strolled hand in hand, momentarily parting to make room for pride-filled mothers chasing after exhilarated children.

"Makhosini, are you there? Can you hear me?" Jerry Goldstein's voice resonated through a Blackberry, and a tall man emerged from the subway stairwell. Four giggling teenage girls in bright sneakers and short shorts halted in the middle of the street.

"Girl, that right there is a fine man!" The girl walking ahead of her friends caught her breath and shouted. Ignoring the screaming traffic, and an angry yellow cab driver hurling insults, the girl's friends erupted into seductive squeals.

"Daddy, you know *you* is fine, right?" the girl shouted more loudly. The man grinned and walked away. "Can I get your number, Daddy? Aw, don't run away."

Disappointed at the man's lack of interest, the nineteen-year-olds delayed traffic as they lazily strolled to a nearby Italian pizzeria.

"Makhosini!" Jerry's voice echoed. "Hey man, can you hear me? Where are you?"

"In Fort Greene." Makhosini visually soaked up the new Fort Greene. A literal taste of Brooklyn's stylish diversity, Fort Greene's residents boasted about their trendy restaurants, quaint cafés, stylish clothing stores, and authentic African-Caribbean cuisine. Rumored to be the heart and soul of Brooklyn's vibrant multi-cultural communities, Fort Greene was truly transforming. "Just got off the Fulton subway."

Makhosini glanced across the street at a clear view of Habana's colorful outpost. Always popular, the place was crowded. He quickly strode past Cake Man Raven's store and heard his stomach growl in anticipation. "That man successfully turned his red velvet cake into a household commodity and a lucrative business. I hear he's now seducing Brooklyn with his blue velvet slices."

"Who's seducing who?" Jerry's excitement seeped through the phone. "You coming, right? This party's started."

"Yeah, I'm almost there. Had to wrap up some things at the office."

"Man, you grinding even on a Saturday." Jerry laughed. "Oh, that reminds me, did your assistant give you the JK Holdings proposal memo from my office?"

"Yep. I received it and read it." Makhosini chuckled at his friend's unwavering persistence.

"It's a great offer. Looks like they really stepped up." Jerry's voice took on a more serious tone as his corporate lawyer side emerged. "So, what are you thinking about their proposal? It's your call, Makhosini."

"I'm thinking it was you who insisted we're not talking business tonight," Makhosini laughed. His eyes shifted to a couple walking in his direction. "Who else is going to be there?"

"Just a few friends. I'll introduce you when you get here." Jerry hung up. Makhosini strolled past Mo's busy bar and entered a quiet side street lined by an endless canopy of flowering trees and Brooklyn's eternal brownstones.

"Man, this is nice." Makhosini's gaze swept over the spacious three-story mansion-style brownstone with ivory walls. Jerry's home resembled the houses featured in Luxury Home magazine. Over the years, Jerry and Tina Goldstein passionately collected large works of art from countries they visited during their marriage. Now that extensive art collection was brazenly displayed throughout their home.

"Five bedrooms and four bathrooms!" Jerry bellowed. "When we bought this place twelve years ago, we paid three hundred grand. By today's market value, it's well over a million. I told you that Fort Greene was coming up, remember?" He proudly grinned at Tina, who disappeared to greet her friends. Makhosini walked farther into the room, concealing his surprise at the sizeable crowd. Jerry's "few friends" turned out to be over a hundred guests comfortably roaming the massive living room and throughout the house.

"You have to help me." Jerry grabbed Makhosini's arm and frantically ushered him to meet his three sisters-in-law. Marsha was an attorney, Mirva an accomplished socialite, and Marilyn a third-year medical student at Columbia University.

"You are single, and they're all still single," Jerry insisted. "Those sisters are practically living in Tina's and my marriage. If you just distract even one of them with your presence, I can live peacefully. Help me escape!"

"What? No." Makhosini laughed at his friend's outrageous plan. "That's not happening, man." Losing himself from Jerry's grip, Makhosini waved at the approaching sisters.

"I'm not dating one of your in-laws so you can live freely," he whispered to Jerry.

"Makhosini, right? It's good to finally meet you. I've heard lots about you from Tina." The woman gently pushed Jerry away. "I'm Marsha, and this is Marilyn and Mirva."

216

"So how did someone like you get involved with Jerry of all people?" Mirva asked. Despite a glimmer of humor in Mirva's green eyes, her voice revealed her disapproval of her brother-in-law.

"He needed at least one friend." Makhosini playfully winked at Mirva, who burst into laughter.

Flabbergasted, Jerry frowned and disappeared.

"So, Tina tells me you own a company, but she never did elaborate on what it is exactly." The pretty Marsha began her interrogation.

"Flame Lilly Consultants," Makhosini announced, settling on a couch next to the sisters. "It's a business strategy company."

"Interesting! Big? Small?" Mirva purred.

"Sorry?" Perplexed by the woman's unconventional approach, Makhosini laughed.

"Would you describe your company as a big or small?" Mirva's lips curled seductively.

"I guess you could say for what we do we're fairly big. Flame Lilly Consultants has thirty-eight employees. Many of our staff have degrees in finance, business administration, or corporate law. We also have two accountants, a statistician, and two data analysts who work directly with our research team."

"Wow!" Marilyn exclaimed, running her nail-bitten fingers through her blonde curls.

"You know, I think I've actually heard of Flame Lilly Consultants!" Marsha exclaimed, her eyes danced in excitement. "It's funny, considering the similarities in our fields of work, I'm really surprised we've never met before. Where did you go to school?"

"University of Sydney," Makhosini said. His eyes shifted to Jerry and Tina dancing in the distance. "I received my Bachelors of Finance there, then stayed on and graduated with an MBA. And you?"

"NYU. New York all the way." Marsha laughed. "Well, I'm glad we've finally met."

"Yes, I agree. It's good to meet you." Mirva's voice softened. Her tall frame relaxed as she leaned closer to Makhosini.

The three women turned out to be as different as they were interesting. Comfortably seated on one end of the sofa, Makhosini sipped on a cold Heineken while listening to their stories.

"You look tired," Marilyn hollered over the music.

"I'm exhausted," he confessed. "The two-week negotiations with JK Holdings were intense, and I'm still jetlagged from yesterday's flight. I think I really should call it a night. Ladies, it was a pleasure meeting you." He slowly rose from the sofa and made his way to the exit.

Time stopped. The room remained frozen as Hugh Masekela's Soweto Blues and a woman in a red dress stole the moment. The music swirled, the woman's red dress flattered. Soweto Blues rattled, she spun. Rhythmically, her shapely legs moved to Hugh's trumpet's sultry seductions. Her arms rose upward. She captured the delicious sounds. Oblivious to appreciative stares, this woman flowed like a waterfall, embracing every note of Hugh's blues.

Captivated, Makhosini stared at the flowing woman. Suddenly, he was an eighteen-year-old boy again, filled with all the longing and desires of boyhood. And the woman in the red dress, she was fifteen again, dancing through time, yet seemingly waiting for this exact

218

moment to begin. When the song ended, her feet stopped. Without hesitation, she walked off the dance area and returned to her seat. The crowd stopped watching, but this woman still held his attention in the arch of her arms.

Familiarity gave birth to confidence. Like a moth drawn to a flame, Makhosini glided to the woman in the red dress until he stood in front of her. Locked in her own thoughts, the woman elegantly crossed her legs, leaned back, and sat comfortably.

"Miss Danai Matamba."

"Eh, hi. . ." she blurted. "Makhosini Moyo?"

They sat side by side, silently stealing glances and sipping glasses of Brotherhood Riesling.

"What? I can't believe this." Danai shook her head and took a long gulp of her sparkling Riesling.

"You look great." Entranced, he stared. *She's changed beautifully yet she's still the same little girl!* "How are you, Little Girl?"

"I'm good," Danai tilted her head. "What are you doing here, Makhosini?"

"I live here." He smiled at her surprise. "Well, in Manhattan on the Upper West Side."

"Really!" Her eyes fluttered in confusion. "Last I heard, you were living in Sydney."

"Yep, I still kind of live there, too." He grinned as the warmth of her gaze invaded his soul. "My company's expanding. I moved here a few years ago when we first opened our New York offices. We're still based in Sydney, and now we have offices in Manhattan and Harare. So, for now, I'm living in all three cities."

"Oh." Her eyes slowly trailed from his eyes, tracing the curve of his jaw and down the rest of body. Without hesitation, she glanced at his left hand searching for a wedding band and looked up curiously when she realized there wasn't one. Makhosini laughed—Danai's eyes still betrayed her every thought.

"And you, Miss Matamba, how have you been? It's been a long time. Are you visiting New York?"

"Actually, I live in an apartment complex around the corner." She giggled.

"Really! So, you know Jerry?"

"No, not really. I know Tina, his wife. We're both members at Gold's Gym, so she invited me." Makhosini glanced up and saw Jerry place his arm over a man's shoulder. Jerry frantically dragged the unsuspecting stranger toward his three sisters-in-law.

"I heard about Flame Lilly Consultants." Danai smiled. She playfully ran her fingers through her braids, causing Makhosini to smile at the unconscious invitation. "Three years ago, Lilly and Godfrey came from Zimbabwe for vacation with their kids. Godfrey mentioned Flame Lilly Consultants. You really did it, Makho!" Her eyes beamed in admiration. His gaze followed her sensual lips and rested on her stubborn high cheek bones. How could he explain this woman sitting next to him? Her smile left him speechless while her laughter playfully stole his attention. She was provocative yet innocent, charming and determined all at once. In this woman's presence, Makhosini Moyo would always remain completely and unapologetically a man.

"I can't believe this! After all these years." Danai laughed. "How are your parents, and oh, how is Sugarbaby?"

"Sugarbaby now prefers to be called Anashe!" Makhosini's lips flickered in amusement. "She celebrated her twenty-fourth birthday earlier this year."

"No, really!" Danai's eyes widen in disbelief.

"Yes, and she constantly reminds me that she's grown up now." He buried his head in his hands then proudly sighed. "Anashe lives and works in Kenya. She loves East Africa. I fly there a couple times a year to check how she's doing." Makhosini momentarily frowned, remembering Anashe's latest confession that she wanted to marry some dude she'd met three months ago.

"What about you, Makhosini, how was Australia? Aah, you just disappeared on everyone." Danai's lips curled in mock disapproval.

"What?" He choked on his Reisling. "Danai, I called you almost every day for a year after I left. You refused to pick the phone. Girl, you gave me a run for my money."

"I was young." She smiled shyly.

"They call that 'stubborn' in the modern world." Makhosini laughed. He looked across the room. In the distance, Jerry desperately placed his arm over a different guy's shoulder. Jerry whispered into the man's ear and introduced him to Marsha. Makhosini chuckled when Tina suddenly appeared and glared at her husband. With surprising swiftness, Tina grabbed Jerry and dragged him away.

"Australia was and still is good, Little Girl. You know, it's funny, a lot of Zimbabweans have moved there, so in many ways it does feel more like home. There's even a Nando's in Sydney!" Makhosini exclaimed. "But I guess a part of me always misses Zimbabwe."

They both sighed at their incurable homesickness. With a forlorn expression, Danai described her unexpected isolation during her first year at university.

"Nothing prepares you for the cultural shock when you move to another country," Makhosini stated, smiling wryly. "It was hard readjusting six years later when Anashe came to live with me. She was an eleven-year-old girl, and I was finishing off my MBA. It felt like I suddenly became a father again. It was difficult." He told Danai about how, determined to find her way in the new world they had entered, Anashe had rebelled against Makhosini. With little thought, he'd insisted on his way. Eventually, an uncomfortable silence took over their tiny apartment. One morning, Makhosini woke up to Anashe crying. She wanted to leave and return home to live with her grandparents. They sat on the floor of their apartment, mourning the things that had fallen apart and trying to make sense of their new life. With tears trailing down his face, Makhosini held his daughter tightly in his arms. That evening, Anashe slept peacefully for the first time since her arrival. The following day, Makhosini had begun readjusting his life to make room for his daughter.

"That's when things started working out. Anashe started liking Australia and making friends. We lived together for almost eight years until she left for university." He shook his head and exhaled.

Danai laughed at his feigned agony. "I bet you miss her every day," she whispered.

"Yeah, I do. I really do." He slowly rose from the sofa and went to bring back a platter of exotic fruits and assorted cheese.

He handed Danai a glass of cherry plum and grinned at her delighted expression.

"We still aim to please!" Makhosini whispered into her ear.

"Hey, Danai, there you are." A male voice invaded their intimacy.

Surprised, Makhosini frowned at the unwelcome intrusion.

"Oh good, I was wondering where you'd disappeared to," the man moved closer.

"Oh hey, where were you? I was looking for you earlier," Danai asked.

"Cupcake Moscato." The man leaned over and handed her a second glass of wine, grinning mischievously.

"Really." Danai sighed appreciatively. "Yes, it's delicious."

Makhosini flinched at the interruption, but neither the intruder nor Danai seemed to notice.

"I'm thinking of leaving in a few." The man adjusted gold cufflinks on his tweed jacket. "Do you want me to drop you off at home?"

"We just got here." A wave of disappointment trailed down Danai's face. "What's up, and where were you anyway?"

"Just went outside to make a call." His eyes flickered in Makhosini's direction before his attention shifted back to his phone. "Mmm, I'll be right back. Have to take this call. Let me know when you're ready to leave, okay?"

"Okay."

"So, is he your man, boyfriend, husband?" Makhosini asked and watched the intruder disappear into Jerry's kitchen.

"What? No." Danai laughed at his wary expression. "That's Charlie! Lillian's younger brother. You remember Uncle Charlie, my mother's

223

youngest sibling. He's here on vacation. He's been staying with me for two weeks."

"Oh." Makhosini grinned boyishly and ran his hand over his hair. "I guess while we are on the topic, I'm curious. Are you married?"

"No," she replied. Several guests screamed with pleasure and rushed to the dance floor. The bodacious sounds of Solly Mahlangu proclaiming "Siyabonga Jesu" drenched the air. Startled, Danai giggled. Makhosini laughed and moved closer to her.

"Hey, how was medical school at UNC Chapel Hill?" he asked, comfortably leaning into the sofa.

"I never went." Danai shrugged her shoulders. Her slender fingers moved to adjust her red shoulder straps.

"What? What do you mean you never went?" His gaze searched her face. "Does that mean you shattered your baba's greatest dream?"

"Yes, I guess I did." Danai winked and laughed at Makhosini's baffled expression. "Yes, I definitely shattered that dream, but he survived. Turned out, I liked Maryland more. So, Morgan State University got me. I majored in architecture."

"What? Really."

"Yes, really." Despite Danai's soft tone, her eyes danced with obvious elation. "I don't save lives, but I get to design and build people's dreams."

"What about your dream?" He glanced up at the increasing crowd. "Do you still do art?"

"Makhosini, you remembered!" Danai's eyes danced in delight. "Yes, I still paint. In fact, there's a huge exhibition this weekend in

Dallas. Two of my works are being displayed alongside four hundred other artists."

"Wow, Miss Matamba! I'm completely impressed." His eyes shone in admiration. He looked out the glass side door at the layers of cherry blossom petals dancing in the wind in Jerry's backyard. "There must have been a lot of pressure on Miles to go to UNC?"

"What, Miles?" Danai rolled her eyes. "Miles jumped ship at the first opportunity! For his sixteenth birthday, he convinced my parents to send him on a short trip to Switzerland. A month later, Miles somehow managed to cross the border to France and get a full scholarship into Le Cordon Bleu Culinary School."

"What!" Makhosini laughed at Miles' mutiny. "So, what happened?"

"That crazy boy called my parents from Paris and said he wasn't coming back home. That was fifteen years ago. My parents are still recovering from the shock!" She shook her head at her brother's antics. "The crazy thing is that Miles grew up to be a wonderful and responsible man. He's now happily married, has two daughters. He owns a restaurant in Harlem on 125th Street—Le Miles!" With pride in her voice, she said, "Can you believe he's a part-time associate professor at the Culinary Institute in a place called Poughkeepsie? It's in upstate New York."

"Your poor father, he never got Chapel Hill." Makhosini wiped tears of laughter from his eyes.

"Oh no, you know Baba always gets what he wants." Danai shook her head in resignation. "A year after Miles escaped to Europe, Baba enrolled *himself* for classes in International Law at UNC Chapel Hill!" Danai reached into her purse and pulled out her phone. Stupefied,

Makhosini gaped at an image of Stan Matamba wearing a tight-fitting sky-blue Tar Heels jersey while confidently posing on Chapel Hill's campus.

"I've never seen Baba so happy. My mother had to fly to North Carolina two years later and literally drag Baba back home. I'm telling you, Makhosini, the craziness is endless. It never stops."

"So, are we leaving?" Charlie returned holding a plate filled with food in one hand and a chicken wing in the other. Danai introduced Makhosini Moyo to her uncle. In the comfort of familiarity, Charlie grinned before reaching into his jacket and answering his phone. "Aah, I have to take this one, too—be back later." He hastily disappeared.

"Are you sure your uncle came from Zimbabwe only two weeks ago?" Makhosini gave her a quizzical look, and she burst into laughter.

Oliver Mtukudzi's soulful voice possessed the atmosphere. "Into Yami," Oliver's voice earnestly professed that all he had belonged to his beloved.

"Ooh, I really love this song," Danai screamed. She raised her arms and rhythmically swayed to the sensuous melody. Suddenly, she stopped moving. Stunned, Danai stared at the middle-aged man standing behind the turntables. "Aah wait! Is that DJ Tonite?" she exclaimed with eyes wide open.

"Yep, that's DJ Tonite," Makhosini grinned.

"Wait, he must be now in his fifties!"

"Yes, he is." Makhosini nodded. "Do you remember Vanessa?"

"Of course I do." A vision of the stiletto-wearing ebony beauty flickered through Danai's mind.

"DJ Tonite's married to Vanessa." Makhosini grinned at Danai's dumbfounded expression. "They live in New Jersey. Tonite works as a tech for an IT company in Manhattan, and he still does music on the side. We sometimes hang out when I'm in New York," Makhosini explained. From behind his spinning turntables, DJ Tonite grinned and raised his champagne glass in their direction.

As Oliver's voice seduced the atmosphere, Makhosini became intoxicated by the soulful music mingled with Danai's delicious laughter. He stared into her eyes. In the heat of her gaze, he became unraveled and began to understand the things he'd never been told. Captured in the moment, he grabbed Danai's hand and led her to the dance area. Without hesitation, she placed her hands around his neck. Makhosini wrapped his arms around her waist and inhaled her flowery scent. He moved closer until the world around them disappeared. In the birth of spring 2012, on a dance floor in Brooklyn, Danai Matamba and Makhosini Moyo began to dance again.